# A Rainbow Over Cuckoo Village

MOONSCION PUBLISHING

'A Rainbow Over Cuckoo Village' 2023

1st edition



Original 'Fairy Stories' cover art by Helen Jacobs: Courtesy Chris Beetles Gallery on behalf of the Helen Jacobs Estate.

Image adapted by Amanda Macias.



ISBN 978-1-7392755-0-1

For information, visit: moonscion.com

The further adventures of
Mirth, Glee, Shimmer & Twinkle and friends
coming soon in –

- The Long Way Home

- Glee & Friends' Book of Silly Poems

# A Rainbow Over Cuckoo Village

PETER MOONSCION

# Contents

*PROLOGUE* ........ *1*

*Chapter 1 Fairies* ........ *14*

*Chapter 2 Cuckoo Village* ........ *17*

*Chapter 3 Mischief Makers* ........ *19*

*Chapter 4 A Rainbow* ........ *25*

*Chapter 5 No School Today* ........ *34*

*Chapter 6 Mysterious Calls* ........ *37*

*Chapter 7 A Drive in the Country* ........ *41*

*Chapter 8 The Quarner Shop* ........ *45*

*Chapter 9 Mr Evan's Eyebrow* ........ *46*

*Chapter 10 A Treasure Cave* ........ *49*

*Chapter 11 The Robinson Family* ........ *53*

*Chapter 12 Shenanigans* ........ *57*

*Chapter 13 In Big Trouble* ........ *65*

*Chapter 14 The Real Oliver* ........ *71*

*Chapter 15 The Sangfroid Family* ........ *77*

*Chapter 16 The Screecher* ........ *81*

*Chapter 17 Patient* ........ *87*

*Chapter 18 A Well-Deserved Whopping* ........ *92*

*Chapter 19 The Vauxhall Family* ........ *96*

*Chapter 20 Victoria Vauxhall* ........................................... *99*

*Chapter 21 Shimmer Meets Vicky* ................................... *100*

*Chapter 22 Green, Red and now. . .* ................................. *105*

*Chapter 23 Flutterby* ........................................................ *110*

*Chapter 24 The Saffron Family* ........................................ *115*

*Chapter 25 Heart of Gold* ................................................. *119*

*Chapter 26 Making Stories* ............................................... *120*

*Chapter 27 The Final Inspection* ...................................... *123*

*Chapter 28 Gathering Together* ........................................ *127*

*Chapter 29 A Short Walk* .................................................. *131*

*Chapter 30 Mrs Abra* ........................................................ *134*

*Chapter 31 A Very Special Guest* ..................................... *139*

*Chapter 32 Where to Sit* ................................................... *141*

*Chapter 33 The Picnic* ...................................................... *144*

*Chapter 34 Butter and Cream* ........................................... *147*

*Chapter 35 The Diagnosis* ................................................ *150*

*Chapter 36 Rumbled* ......................................................... *153*

*Chapter 37 Wiseacre and Mrs Abra* ................................. *155*

*Chapter 38 Good Old-Fashioned Wisdom* ....................... *157*

*Chapter 39 Reverse Alchemy* ........................................... *159*

*Chapter 40 How to Stop a Volcano* .................................. *165*

*Chapter 41 Higher Magic* ................................................. *171*

*Chapter 42 The First is Last* ............................................. *174*

*Chapter 43 Is that It?*......................................................177
*Chapter 44 Story Time*......................................................179
*Chapter 45 Jenny's Turn*......................................................181
*Chapter 46 Smiling Faces*......................................................183
*Chapter 47 Maybel's Visit*......................................................190
*Chapter 48 Picnic's End*......................................................193
*Chapter 49 Goodbyes*......................................................196
*Chapter 50 Home Time*......................................................203
*Chapter 51 Going Home*......................................................210
*Chapter 52 Away with the Fairies*......................................................211
*EPILOGUE*......................................................215
*1 How do I do?*......................................................215
*2 Anywhen*......................................................217
*3 The Beginning*......................................................222

PROLOGUE

# Buttercup

Here is the story of four mischievous little fairies and the trouble they caused on their day off.

I'd like to say that I wrote this story, but the truth is, I didn't. I found it. That's right, I found this story, and you'll never guess of all the places that you can think of where a person might 'find' a story.

*(Editor's note: Thomas didn't find the story. I did.)*

*(My note on my editor's note: we can let the dear reader decide who found the story Emily).*

*(Editors second note: Ok, but I found it.)*

Well anyway, here is what happened.

When I was a child, my younger sister Emily (who is helping me to write this down) and I often had picnics at the bottom of our garden.

One summer's day we were having a picnic together in the garden. It was just lunch really but as usual we had asked our mother to pack the jam and also peanut butter sandwiches, apples, cakes and orange juice into the picnic basket so we could take it into the garden with a blanket and eat it as a picnic.

Every time we had a picnic, we used to tell each other stories because we loved stories so much. We loved the ones we had learned, and we also loved to make them up. The bottom of the garden was mine and Emily's special picnic and story place. We loved stories so much that once, after it had started to rain, we didn't leave the garden to go inside until we had finished the story. We would rather have been soaked in the rain than have the story interrupted. Maybe that's why we found this one. Because we loved stories so much, it just had to come to us.

In fact, the only time we ever failed to finish a story when playing in the garden was one cold winter's day after there had been lots of snow. We were building a snowman (where else but at the bottom of our garden) and rolled a large snowball to make the snowman's body. I had started to tell Emily a story, and by the time we had finished the snowman, I was only halfway through when it started to snow again. Our mum called out for us to come inside and that she had made hot chocolate for us. So, as we were very cold and also really, really loved hot chocolate, we reluctantly agreed to finish the story inside.

We ran to the house and just as we were about to open the door to go inside, we heard the sound of thunder. We both had the same thought 'it thunders when it's raining, not when it's snowing'. Then we looked up and just at that moment all the snow that had built up on top of the awning above the door suddenly slid off in one great avalanche and was dumped all over Emily and I. Hearing my 'Arrhhhhh' and Emily's loud 'Squeeek' as the snow piled onto us, our mother rushed out to see what had happened. When she opened the door, she found the two of us looking like a snow boy and snow girl waiting to be let inside. All Emily said was "Hmmfff, if we'd finished the story, we wouldn't have been on this spot at this very moment." After that, we promised each other to never let a picnic story go unfinished.

We loved picnics the most when our mum and dad were there; especially because we could pester them to tell us a story. When they were too busy, it was just me and my sister; who was just one year younger than me and 'almost' as good at telling stories.

*(Editors third note: Hmphh, you mean 'better'.)*

*(My note to editors third note: Stop making editors notes Emily, it's interrupting the story.)*

*(Editors fourth note: Then stop writing silly things.)*

*(My note to editors fourth note: Ok I'll try.)*

Now where was I? Oh yes, on the day that we found the story, we were enjoying our picnic and Emily had finished telling me a story she had made up. It was about a king and queen long ago who loved butter and also buttercups.

The King and Queen loved buttercups so much that they told everyone they could not use money anymore and had to use buttercups instead. That way, people would grow buttercups everywhere and whenever they bought something, they would have to pay for it in buttercups. The King and Queen would then see buttercups wherever they went and people would always be giving each other buttercups.

It was said too that every day the King and Queen would hold a buttercup under each other's chin to check if they still loved butter and buttercups. The way to tell being, whether or not the yellowy-gold colour from the buttercup reflected onto their chin.

In fact, the King used to have a big, bushy beard but

his beloved Queen had complained that she couldn't check if he still loved buttercups because his beard was in the way, so, he shaved it off. Until then, almost all the men in the kingdom used to have beards, but when the king stopped growing a beard, all the other men in his kingdom copied his new style and shaved off their beards too; and all because of buttercups.

I had added that I personally thought that when the king gave the Queen a kiss it was itchy, so she was probably happy for him to shave off his beard for that reason too. Then Emily had told me to be quiet as it was her story and only she was allowed to decide what happens.

After she finished telling me the story, Emily then leaned over and picked a buttercup from the grass. She asked me if I believed the story and I said that I did. She then asked me if I liked butter and I answered that I did.

Then I laughed and added "especially if it was on top of a scone and under some Jam." Emily giggled at this then said that the only way to find out if someone really liked butter as well as buttercups was to hold a freshly picked buttercup under their chin to see if the gold colour reflected onto their chin.

She didn't mention that she had made that up in the story she had only just told me, and instead acted as if she had always known it and only silly people didn't know that.

Emily then told me to put my head back but didn't wait for me to do so as she pushed it back herself. She then placed the buttercup under my chin and asked me in a serious voice "Thomas, do you like butter and buttercups?"

"Yes I do" I answered.

She then carefully checked to see if the gold colour from the buttercup had reflected onto my chin, and squealing with delight, she exclaimed. "You do! You do like butter."

"I told you I do" I said, quickly getting up as I was eager to test if she also liked butter and buttercups.

I took the buttercup from her, but I didn't need to tell her to put her head back. She quickly leaned back with her elbows on the grass in her eagerness for it to be confirmed that she liked butter and buttercups.

"Say ahhhh" I joked as I lifted the buttercup to her chin.

"You're not a doctor" she complained.

Then, "get on with it," she bossed.

So I did, and holding the buttercup under her chin, I asked her the same question. "Emily, do you like butter and buttercups?"

"Yes, I do like butter and buttercups." She said solemnly as if giving an oath.

Then she added with a giggle, "especially if it's peanut butter."

Peanut butter was her favourite. She was crazy about it. She was always being told off for dipping her finger into the jar and eating the peanut butter from it as if it was a lollipop.

I held the buttercup under her chin and looked very closely to see if the gold colour reflected onto her chin. It did.

"You do too!" I said at the discovery.

"Really?" She asked excitedly while keeping still and not moving her head away so the gold colour would stay longer on her chin.

"Is my chin very, very golden?" she pestered.

"Yes it is," I answered.

I then took an even closer look as the bright sunshine reflected off the buttercup in a golden glow under her chin.

"It's so golden" I said.

Emily squealed with delight again but made no attempt to move her head away from the buttercup that I was still gently holding under her chin.

"I wish I could lay down on a sunny day in a field so full of buttercups and be shinning gold all over. I'd stay there sooo long that when I went away, I'd still be golden for ever and ever amen."

I was going to move the buttercup away from her chin but she cried and begged me not to.

"Nooooooo keep it there, pleeeeaase," She whined.

She told me she wanted to see if I held it there for a long time if the underside of her chin would stay golden coloured.

I agreed and held the buttercup in place under her chin. After a while, my arm grew tired and even though it was only a tiny buttercup, I had to hold it under her chin with both hands. Time went by and I wanted to take the buttercup away but Emily whined at me to "please, please, please, pleeeease just hold it there a little longer, please, please, pleeeease."

I said I would again and as I was a little bored, I decided to count the petals on the buttercup.

"How many petals do you think the buttercup has" I asked.

"I'm sorry, I'm busy butter-bathing at the moment, I

can't think" came Emily's ungrateful answer.

I decided to count them for my own curiosity, and the buttercup had five golden petals. But there was something more interesting than about this particular buttercup.

With my head so close to the little golden flower, I noticed something very curious indeed. I was not an expert on the subject of buttercups. In fact, I don't think I'd ever picked or held or even thought about one before that moment. But there was something strange about this particular buttercup; something very strange. Strange and, as I was soon to discover, wonderfully magical.

As I lay on my belly in the cool grass with my head under Emily's chin counting the petals of the buttercup, I had noticed that all five petals were pretty much the same shape, the same size and the same yellowy/golden colour. Then, as I tilted the buttercup to catch the sun to reflect onto Emily's chin, I noticed that there was an unusual pattern on the inside of each petal. I looked closer and closer. I looked as close as I could until just before I became cross-eyed. The pattern was so tiny that I couldn't see the details of it clearly.

The buttercup was tiny, the petals were even tinier and the pattern on the inside of each petal was incredibly tiny. The reason the pattern seemed strange and out of place to me was that it was all straight lines and squares. Everything else in nature was usually swirly. So, I decided to investigate with my magnifying glass.

Forgetting about poor butter-bathing Emily, I moved away from her chin with the buttercup and reached for my backpack which had all the essential things a boy needs. It had my comics, toy soldiers, a penknife and among other things, it had my magnifying glass.

I loved my magnifying glass most of all, as I liked to examine tiny creatures which grew much bigger when seen through the glass. A spider spinning a web on the branches of a bush, an oozing snail making its slow way across the garden as it leaves an icky, sticky trail; or a toodling ladybird munching at leaves here and there before flying off. They would all become huge and scary when seen through my magnifying glass.

"Heyyyy!" Protested Emily at the disturbance to her butter bathing.

"Sorry" I said absent mindedly, as I began to examine the buttercup with the magnifying glass.

It was no use though. The patterns were so small that even with the magnifying glass, I couldn't make out the details.

I explained the mystery to Emily.

"It's mine, I picked it" She instantly squealed, laying claim to whatever it was that I might unravel.

*(Editors' final note: See, I found it).*

*(My final note to the editor's final note: So you did, but I found the story).*

*(Editors final, final note: Hmphh).*

Continuing the story about finding the story.

I told Emily I still couldn't see the pattern clearly with the magnifying glass.

"Your microscope!" she guessed correctly.

I had examined everything imaginable with my microscope. From making tiny bugs seem like giant monsters, to marvelling at the simple things in life such as a grain of sand or a hair from Emily's head; usually snatched without permission followed by a loud 'Oi'.

Here though was a real challenge.

We abandoned the unfinished food to the ants and hurried to my room. After all, we had a rule that we couldn't leave a story unfinished, but lunch was a different matter.

It didn't take long to set up, and as soon as I peered into the microscope and brought the buttercup petals into focus, I saw the most magical thing ever.

On the upper side of each of the five golden petals of the buttercup were the smallest, tiniest, most minuscule letters, words and sentences ever possible in the world. The petals were arranged, one after the other, just like the pages of a book. And on them were tiny, tiny, tiny, beautifully handwritten letters. I couldn't believe it and had to look back a few times to check if I was dreaming. Emily looked and couldn't believe it too.

We didn't have time to waste as we were worried the buttercup would wilt and we might lose the tiny writing. We decided to take it in turns to copy all the words down and to read them afterwards, but it was going to take a long time because there was a lot of them. We also couldn't read the buttercup like a book because the microscope was zoomed in so close. So, we had to move over the words carefully one letter at a time.

It took a long, long time and our whole bodies began to ache as the minutes turned into hours. Our excitement remained though, so despite the discomfort, we kept at it until the laborious task was done.

Letter by letter, word by word, sentence by sentence, paragraph by paragraph and page by page, we each took turns in reading out loud what we saw through the microscope as the other repeated it to be sure as they wrote it down.

"Capital A"

"Capital A" confirmed Emily as she took the first turn at writing.

"Space" I continued.

"Space" Emily dutifully repeated.

"Capital R"

"Capital R"

"a"

"a"

"i"

"i"

"n"

"n"

"b"

"b"

"o"

"o"

"w"

"w"

"Space"

"Space"

"Capital O"

"Capital O"

"v"

"v"

"e"

"e"

“r”

“r”

And so on, all the way until we reached the very last full stop on the very last sentence on the fifth and last petal of the whole thing.

I'm sure even reading the first part that way gets boring after a while. Well, there were hundreds of thousands of letters for us to read and write down, and it took ever such a long time. We had to fib to Mother that we had some terribly hard homework to finish; otherwise she might have thought we'd been kidnapped by aliens or something.

Despite the hard work, we were desperately eager to read what the letters spelled out. We were patient though and kept at the task and the closer we got to the end, the more excited we became. Sometimes as I read out the letters one by one to Emily, I found myself trying to remember what the earlier ones had been so as to guess what some of the words and sentences might say. I took the time I had to wait while Emily wrote down each letter I had just recited to try to work them out, but as I did so, I would forget my place and Emily started getting cross with me.

Emily might have been a year younger than I, but one thing you don't want in our family is a 'cross' Emily. I quickly decided that the safest course would be to try to be patient and just concentrate on getting the letters in the right order.

After we copied everything down, we finally got to read it and it was, of all things, a story. It was fairy story called ‘A Rainbow Over Cuckoo Village’ and it was written by someone who signed their name mysteriously as just ‘W’ who we thought must be a fairy because the story is about fairies.

We mainly thought it must have been written by a fairy because it was handwritten in tiny, minuscule, beautiful letters on the petals of a buttercup.

We don't know why we found it. Maybe it was because we loved stories so much. Maybe fairies enjoyed listening to our picnic stories and wanted to tell us one. Maybe they had left them there for us before and we had never found them because they were so tiny.

Whatever the reason, we were so happy to find a lovely story in such a magical way. We looked many times after that in many places and on the petals of other flowers too such as daises and my favourite which are dandelions, but we never found another one. Perhaps it is only once in a lifetime that we could find something so wonderful and magical.

We didn't mind not finding any more stories though. As well as being a lovely story it was also kind of magical because, after we read it to each other, we soon started to feel ourselves forgetting it. So the next time we read it or listened to it being read, it sounded like a new story again. If we didn't tell it to each other for a long time, we almost forgot it completely so could enjoy it as if it was a brand-new story.

One time, we totally forgot about the story, and when we found it written down in our own handwriting we were surprised. Of course, we enjoyed reading it out loud over our next picnic and it was only when we got to the end that we remembered finding it and writing it out. We wondered if a fairy might have put a forgetting spell on the story, but that's silly . . . isn't it?

We were just happy that we could enjoy it again and again as if it were a new story. Haven't you ever read a book that was so wonderful, yet felt a little sad when you came to the end because you have to say goodbye to the story, and even if you do read it again it's never quite the same because it isn't surprising and new? Well, if you almost forget the story, or don't read it for many, many years then it can be wonderful when you read it again.

Until now, we have kept the story secret and just re-told it to each other. But perhaps, one day someone will find the book we wrote it in just as we found it on the petals of a buttercup and they might publish it for all children to read.

Wc worricd that thc fairics might havc cxpcctcd us to keep the story a secret forever. But surely, they would want many people to enjoy such a lovely story. They wouldn’t be concerned about being exposed, as most readers probably wouldn’t believe the part about fairies leaving the story on the petals of a buttercup. They would think we just made it up. That’s ok though. The most important thing is that the story is enjoyed, and the more people who enjoy it, the happier we will be.

So, here is the story that we found one day while having a picnic. You can decide for yourself if it is true or just made up.

# A Rainbow Over Cuckoo Village

By W.

## CHAPTER 1

## Fairies

Fairies work very, very hard.

All day long, and sometimes at night, they go around, sometimes visible and sometimes invisible, casting spells and working magic.

When they are visible, fairies always try to avoid being seen. That's why people almost never catch sight of one. That's when they cast the kind of spells or work magic that makes the world we live in so beautiful and, well, magical.

That's when they work their magic on the world and leave it for us to find later and enjoy. I'm sure you can think of a time that you saw something that you thought looked so wonderful that it was 'more' than beautiful . . . it was magical.

Perhaps it was one day when you woke up in the morning and found that it was snowing and everything outside was blanketed in white, fluffy snow. Maybe it was when you picked a dandelion and blew on it, and all the seeds puffed into the air and drifted away. Or perhaps when you looked over that same field the next day and saw a hundred more dandelions.

Or maybe it was when it was a rainy day, and you felt a little sad. Then suddenly, a cloud moved, and a golden beam of sunlight broke through and brightened everything up so much and looked so beautiful that you forgot that you were sad.

Or maybe, just like me, you sometimes see a rainbow and that's all you need because everyone knows that rainbows are one of the most beautiful and magical things in the whole world.

Well, whatever it was that looked magical to you, that was probably one of the things that fairies made when they were visible and were sure that no human would spot them as they worked hard to leave something for you to enjoy.

When fairies create something beautiful for you to experience, your appreciation and joy is a kind of nourishment for them. So, while you consume food for your bodies and love for your hearts, fairies are nourished by the happiness that humans feel when they enjoy the beauty and magic the fairies have created.

When they are invisible, fairies don’t need to worry about being spotted by humans, so they can go anywhere at any time. That’s when they work their magic on people.

One day a person might do something so kind or funny, or so magical, or say something that is so wise that it makes people very happy. I’m sure you can think of an occasion when someone was very kind or did something that you thought was magical. Well, at that time, there was probably a fairy whispering in their ear.

Fairies are always good and always kind, and it’s very unusual indeed to hear of a fairy being naughty or misbehaving. Sometimes though, it does happen, and when it does, it's almost always on the rare occasion that they have a day off from their work. That's why in fact they very rarely have a day off. fairies have lots and lots of energy and always like to be busy. When they do have a day off, they sometimes become restless and get up to mischief, especially youngling fairies.

This is the story of what happened when four young fairies had a day off and decided very early in the morning to play together. Of course, being young fairies, having free time that day and lots and lots of energy, they decided to get up to mischief and to play a naughty trick on some humans.

CHAPTER 2

# Cuckoo Village

The humans the four fairy friends chose to play the trick on, were the people who lived in a beautiful but tiny place in the countryside called 'Cuckoo Village'.

Cuckoo Village was so small that some people said it wasn't even a village at all. The village only had one street and was by a stream which separated it from a grassy hill where Farmer Crabtree's cows spent most of their day hanging around eating grass. When they weren't munching at the grass, they sniffed and snuffled curiously at anything on the ground that wasn't grass.

The village only had twelve little houses, one small shop (which was really just one of the houses with a sign stuck to the wall) and a lovely little church that was even older than Crabtree Farm and which only held a service on special holidays such as Christmas or Easter.

Old Mr and Mrs Evans ran the shop part time and lived above it. The shop, which sold all those little things that you always seemed to forget to buy when you had been to the supermarket, was so small inside that it was only really half a shop.

Some of the people from nearby villages and towns sometimes said that eleven and a half houses and half a shop, and a part time shop at that, were not enough to make a village.

The villagers didn't pay any attention to that though. As far as they were concerned any group of houses close together, with a shop, even if it was only half a shop and open only part time, and a church, even if it was only open for special holidays . . . was a village.

Besides, there was a sign on the road that read 'Cuckoo Village' and you might argue with people, but you just can't argue with a sign now, can you?

Also, the only thing smaller than a village is a hamlet; the difference being that a village has a church and a hamlet does not. The church in Cuckoo Village didn't have a vicar, but Reverend Smiley from Plumton always came at Christmas and Easter or for a rare wedding or Christening. So, even though the sleepy church was closed most of the time, it was still there. So that made Cuckoo Village a village. After all, 'Cuckoo Hamlet' just doesn't sound right, does it?

The reason the four fairies chose the people of Cuckoo Village to play their trick on was that it had been raining during the night and early that morning there was a beautiful rainbow stretching right over and into the village.

Fortunately for the four youngling fairies, and unfortunately for the people of Cuckoo village, a rainbow is exactly what they needed to make their 'day off' magic work.

CHAPTER 3

# Mischief Makers

Fairies can work all kinds of wonderful and powerful magic, but when they want to play a trick or do something naughty it isn't as easy for them. To work naughty magic, they need to study very hard and also first have to perform a difficult task. If they do the task well, then they can cast a mischievous spell.

These particular mischievous fairies were called Mirth, Glee, Shimmer and Twinkle.

Mirth, a very kind fairy, is a little bit older and wiser than the others and is the leader. Mirth doesn't always express his emotions as he is often deep in thought, but his friends can always feel his warm heart and love for them.

Glee is always very happy and loves to sing and tell stories and make his friends laugh, and is Mirth's best friend. Despite being an amiable and very friendly fairy, Glee is always happy to join the others in some mischievous adventure.

Shimmer is said to be the prettiest fairy any other fairy had ever seen, but she thinks that's silly and not important at all. Oh and, Shimmer also has the loveliest singing voice of all fairies. So, when Glee writes a song, he usually asks her to sing it. This is because, although he likes to sing, Glee prefers to hear his songs sung by Shimmer.

Twinkle is a very, very cute fairy but also feisty and

strong willed - especially when she is protecting someone. Twinkle is liked by all fairies, but they are always a little careful what they say and do around her as they know better than to cross her. Twinkle is Mirth's baby sister and Shimmer's best friend.

Mirth, Glee, Shimmer and Twinkle love each other very much and always work and play together. So, if they were going to do something naughty (which wasn't often) and maybe even get into trouble, they even wanted to do that together.

On that day, Mirth told his three friends that he wanted to play a trick on the people of Cuckoo Village. As soon as they heard this, they became excited and had begged him to let them join in. Mirth had agreed and told them that each must choose a human child from the village to play the trick on. Mirth and Glee were boy fairies so they would choose a little boy each. Shimmer and Twinkle were girl fairies so they would choose a little girl each to play the trick on.

When they asked Mirth what the trick would be exactly, he wouldn't tell them and said it would be a surprise even to them, so they would have to wait to see it for themselves.

"Sometimes telling is better than showing and sometimes showing is better than telling," Mirth had said. Then he added with a teasing smile "in this case showing is better, so you'll know when you see."

Shimmer, Twinkle and Glee, being fairies, loved surprises so squeaked with joy. Although they still couldn't resist pestering Mirth to tell them what the trick would be. Mirth loved attention, so he planned to wait until the very last moment to tell them anything so they'd have to keep pestering him. He told them that the only clue he would give is that they needed a village with a rainbow overhead that also had children living there and it just so happens that a rainbow was going to appear over Cuckoo Village that morning.

That wasn't much of a clue and didn't help as they weren't as experienced as Mirth in casting 'naughty' spells. Naughty spells were so complicated and didn't come as naturally as the normal kind, so most fairies didn't bother to take the time to learn them. Still, the friends didn't mind waiting to see for themselves what the trick would be.

They had lots of fun trying to guess what it was that the spell would do and why it was that they needed a rainbow of all things.

Mirth did however tell them what the difficult task was that they would have to perform in order to make the naughty spell work.

The others listened carefully while he told them that they had to 'loop the loop' around a rainbow.

"What's looby loo?" asked Shimmer.

"Not looby loo . . . loop the loop" answered Glee. Then, "It's when you fly and do a loop up, over, down and straight again. A loop" he further explained as he waved his finger in a circle.

"Ha, that's easy. I could do that since I was little" boasted Twinkle. She then flew in three loops in a row to prove it.

"You still are little" said a smiling Mirth to his baby sister as he hovered over to her. Then, "but have you ever looped a rainbow?" he asked.

"Well, no, how can you, they always run away when

you try to get near. I know cause I've tried. . . a LOT" Twinkle laughed.

"She has" nodded a wide eyed Shimmer confirming the 'a lot' part of Twinkle's statement.

Twinkle was right. This may sound like an easy task for fairies. After all, they can fly. However, if you have ever noticed, it is almost impossible to get close to a rainbow. Every time you move close to one, it seems to move to another place, and even though fairies 'can' fly and are magical, it is just the same for them.

Twinkle, Shimmer and Glee looked at each other puzzled and wondered how it could be done. They had enjoyed the beautiful sight of a rainbow many times, but whenever they had flown towards one, they never seemed to get any closer as it always moved away as they approached it.

They had also never met a fairy who was responsible for making rainbows so they couldn't ask them about it. Rainbow makers were very, very senior fairies and youngling fairies didn't come across senior fairies too often let alone a very, very senior fairies. At least, they didn't come across very, very senior fairs and know it. Some said that the highest of senior fairies were just as invisible to youngling fairies as all fairies are to humans. So they might have come across them withing realising it.

Mirth didn't look worried by the problem of how to approach a rainbow though, and he told them proudly that, 'he didn't want to go into detail, but he'd had 'dealings' with rainbows in the past'.

Then, with a very serious and solemn look on his face, he told them that he would teach them how to approach a rainbow, but only if they would cross their heart and promise by bluebells, foxgloves and snapdragons to never ever tell it to anyone else or do it without Mirth's permission.

All three quickly crossed their heart and nodded as they promised never to tell anyone else the secret. And just to be double sure that Mirth would agree to teach them, Shimmer put her hands together and said "please, please, pleeeeeease teach us Mirthy, I won't tell anyone else in the whole wide world. I double promise by bluebells, foxgloves and snapdragons"

Mirth looked at all three, one after the other to show them that he was serious, and to make them think he still hadn't decided if he was going to teach them or not even though he had already decided he would.

Finally, he nodded slowly and said, "very well, I will teach you."

This time all three threw their arms in the air in celebration and Twinkle couldn't contain her joy so she did another three loops on the spot.

"Wheeeeeeee" she squealed as she looped around and around.

When Shimmer and Glee had calmed down, and Twinkle had gotten as calm as it was reasonable to expect, Mirth flew close to each of his friends, and one by one, he whispered the secret of how to get close to a rainbow.

As he did so, and without them noticing, he cast a little spell on each of them that would make them forget the secret as soon as they had used it.

After all, it was a very valuable secret and he had studied hard to learn it. Mirth thought such powerful magic secrets were best understood when the fairy who knew them had studied hard and practiced well to learn them. But, for their task today he was willing to 'lend' the secret to his friends, but not let them keep it. The forgetting spell would take care of that very nicely indeed.

Having received (for now) the secret of how to approach a rainbow, the four fairies were ready for a day of mischief. So, with Mirth leading and Glee, Shimmer and Twinkle following, they set off in the direction of Cuckoo Village.

CHAPTER 4

# A Rainbow

Mirth, Glee, Shimmer and Twinkle all noticed Farmer Crabtree and his dog Nuzzler standing in his cow field looking up at the rainbow.

They were bursting with energy in their excitement at the mischievous trick they were preparing and were glowing brightly. However, even though they were doing the kind of magic that fairies do when they are visible, they didn't worry about being spotted by the farmer. The fairies guessed correctly that he, and his dog, would just think they were fireflies, even if it was morning time. After all, that's why fairies had made fireflies in the first placc. So that if humans ever did see a fairy when they were visible, they could just pretend to be a firefly.

After using Mirth's secret to approach the rainbow, they all followed him in trying to loop the loop around it.

Even Mirth didn't get it quite right the first time. Sometimes, even when you know how to do something, it still takes a little practice to get it right. So, he led them again and again until they all got it right together and one after the other, all four friends could complete a perfect loop around the rainbow as it stretched all the way over and into Cuckoo Village.

Once they accomplished this, Mirth ordered each of them to move into the rainbow; each at different colour bands.

First, Mirth moved into the green band within the

rainbow. Then he told Glee to move into the red band and he did so.

When Glee entered the rainbow and settled into its red band, a look of wonder came over him as he hovered within the brightest, reddest light he had ever seen.

Next, Mirth called out to Shimmer and told her to go into the blue band of the rainbow. Shimmer looked in awe at how green Mirth appeared and how red Glee looked. She wasn't afraid as both looked as happy as can be to hover inside the rainbow. But it was something new for her, so she hesitated for a moment until her friend twinkle placed her hands on her back and gave her a long, hard shove towards the blue band.

"In you go," laughed Twinkle.

"Hey!" complained Shimmer with a laugh. Then "Ooooooo, it's so. . . awwww."

"Isn't it? nodded Glee happily.

"Me, me, my turn" shouted Twinkle.

"You don't have to shout Twinks, it's not a window," teased a very happy Shimmer from within her bright blue band of the rainbow.

"Ok Twinkle, you go into the yellow band," said Mirth.

With an excited "woo hoo," Twinkle was already eagerly flying head-on at the rainbow as soon as Mirth said 'ok'. She then made a sudden course correction as soon as she heard what her colour band would be. She was flying too fast though, and in her excitement she pooft right through and out the other side of the rainbow. Her friends just looked at her, all three slowly shook their heads as if to say 'that's Twinkle'.

When she realised she had overshot her mark, she

stopped then slowly hovered backwards until she was in place within the rainbow's yellow band in the hope that no one had noticed.

"Yeah, we all saw that Twinks" said Shimmer.

Twinkle just shrugged her shoulders and gave an embarrassed grin.

"Ohhhh, it's all yellowy!" said Twinkle in wonder.

Then, to make it so Shimmer was wrong and not herself for overshooting the rainbow, she complained, "hey Shims, you're supposed to be in blue not green.

"I am in blue" said Shimmer looking at Twinkle as if she was dreaming.

"Oh, you are definitely in green," she insisted. Then turning to Glee she said "isn't she Gle . . . hey why are you in orange? Ha, I might have 'over-landed' but at least I got the right colour."

"Ha, 'over-landed', that's a good-un Twinkle," laughed Glee.

"They are in their right colours Twinkle," assured Mirth. Then, "you are in yellow so you are seeing Shimmer through yellow, green and blue light so she looks green. And you are seeing Glee through yellow and red so he looks orange.

Twinkle was about to complain that although this made sense, the way they looked to her was what mattered, but Mirth cut her off as it was time to complete the spell.

"Ok, hold your positions, this is the most important part" he said urgently as he turned to face the rising sun.

Until that moment, the rainbow was faint as the sun had just started to peek over the distant hills to the east beyond nearby Plumton. Although the first partial appearance of the sunrise had given enough love to create the rainbow, it was only when the whole sun had sailed over the horizon that all of its light could flood into the rainbow and power the spell that Mirth was working.

Mirth and his three friends turned to face eastward just as the full force of the sun's golden rays poured into the rainbow. All four fairies gasped as they felt ever more sparkling, glittering, magical power arcing along all of the rainbow's colour bands and through their hearts.

For a moment, it was as if they became one with the rainbow. The sun-charged energy of its colour bands infused them with the rainbow's magical beauty and each of them absorbed all the power of the band that surrounded and embraced them.

They all cheered as they could feel they had the power to finally cast their spell; even if it was a naughty one.

Satisfied with the proceedings, Mirth hovered in place in the green band of the rainbow and reached into the blue band and took Shimmer by the hand. Then he turned to his left and joined hands with Twinkle. Twinkle then guessed correctly that Mirth wanted them all to join hands, so she reached into the red band of the rainbow and grabbed Glee's hand without waiting for him to offer it.

"Ready" said Mirth as he looked towards Cuckoo Village which was along and down at the very end of the rainbow's arc.

"Ready" they all said in anticipation of what came next.

At this, Mirth went into a dive through the rainbows colour band as he swooped towards the village. As they were all holding hands, the others were pulled along but soon joined Mirth in his enthusiastic dive downward.

Already charged with the power of his chosen colour band, Mirth felt like he was scooping up ever more energy from his colour band as he dove faster and faster down the rainbow's arc. And he was, just as his friends Glee, Shimmer and Twinkle were too.

Glee, Shimmer and Twinkle felt the same with their red, blue and yellow colour bands, and for a moment the firefly glow of all four fairy friends took on the colour they were bathed in.

As they drew closer to Cuckoo Village, Mirth pulled upwards a little and they exited the rainbow as it fell away from them and illuminated the still sleepy houses of the village.

The four friends hovered for a moment in readiness for their mischief. Twinkle looked over at her friend Shimmer with amazement. Shimmer was totally completely blue. She had blue hair, blue eyes, blue teeth and even blue fingernails.

Shimmer noticed Twinkle staring at her and she looked back with equal amazement. Twinkle was totally, completely golden yellow. She had golden yellow hair, golden yellow eyes, golden yellow teeth and even golden yellow finger nails.

Then both of them looked over to Mirth and Glee who of course stared back at them. All of the four fairy friends had absorbed the beauty of the rainbow. As they had left it behind, the unusual effect on their outer form started to fade, but they still felt it present within as it was now entangled with the mischievous magic they were about to perform.

After all, magic may seem simple and easy when the

results are enjoyed, be even fairy magic has a process and a way of being prepared, and what better ingredients for fairy magic could there be than the power and beauty of a rainbow.

Soon after they left the rainbow and set off on their way down to Cuckoo Village, Glee, Shimmer and Twinkle started to forget the secret of how to approach and loop the loop around a rainbow.

Not only did they forget the secret, but they also forgot that they had ever known it. So, they would never ask themselves the question, ‘Mmmm, how is it that I was able to approach and loop the loop around the rainbow and now can’t remember how to do it? Mirth must have cast a spell on me to make me forget it’. Then, they would pester Mirth to tell them all over again how to get close enough to loop rainbow. This way though, Mirth's spell not only made them forget the secret, but also made them forget that they ever knew it so they wouldn’t pester him about it. After all, he liked their attention on most things, but he liked his secrets even more and guarded them carefully.

Unfortunately, ‘I’ also don’t know the secret of how to approach a rainbow and how to loop the loop around them. So, I can’t tell you. At least, I don’t know now, and I don’t remember ever knowing. Though, I might have known and somehow forgotten, and even forgotten that I ever knew.

I do have four guesses though. And of course, they are just guesses.

One way might be for a fairy to learn to fly faster than the speed of light. That's because rainbows are made of different colours of light and if you fly at them faster than light then the rainbow wouldn't be quick enough to move away before you got to it.

Of course, flying faster than the speed of light would make it difficult to come to a sudden stop, fly straight up, over and then down again (which is what you would have to do to make a loop). Besides, that sounds all very technical, doesn't it? And fairies usually do things by an even higher kind of magic than science, so that's the least favourite of my guesses.

My second guess would be if the fairy kept very quiet and moved very, very slowly, it might be able to sneak up to the rainbow. This is because rainbows must be ever so shy as whenever anyone tries to go near them, they move away. Try it, when you are walking or driving in the countryside and there is a rainbow that you think you are getting closer to, it always moves away. If you walked very slowly though, and kept very, very quiet, it might not move.

The third guess I have is if the fairy found a colour that wasn't in the rainbow, and disguised itself as that colour and then approached the rainbow slowly and tried to convince it that, 'I'm very sorry but I got lost and was supposed to be part of the rainbow and look see, you don't have my colour do you.' The rainbow would then invite the disguised fairy in and as it got closer, it could suddenly do a loop around it. The problem with this guess is that I don't really know if there are any colours that exist that are not already in rainbows. They might exist somewhere, but I have never seen one. If anyone can find one though, a fairy can.

My fourth, and favourite guess is that a fairy who

knew advanced spells could see where a rainbow is, then cast a time travel spell. They would then go back in time to wait at the place where the rainbow is going to appear. That way, the rainbow comes to him or her rather than them having to go to the rainbow.

Of course, young fairies can't time travel but there are stories about senior fairies going both back 'and' forward in time, and if I ever come across one then I'll ask if they have ever met a rainbow.

One of these could be the way to approach a rainbow before it moves away. Or, there may be another way. I wish I knew. I even wish that I used to know. But I just don't remember ever knowing.

Glee, Shimmer and Twinkle used to know, but now they have forgot, and they don't even remember that they have forgot. Only Mirth remembers that.

Before they went down to visit the Cuckoo children, they had chosen for themselves to cast their mischievous spells on, Mirth told them the only rule.

"Once your spell is cast, you can't interfere with the results" he warned

Glee, Shimmer and Twinkle nodded their acceptance.

Mirth continued in a serious tone "you can watch and enjoy the fun and even stir up more trouble, but you can't help to reverse the spell or change it in any way."

Again they agreed with even Twinkle showing how seriously she was taking Mirth's warning.

"Once the powerful magic has started having its effect, things have to be allowed to sort themselves out naturally" Mirth concluded in a serious whisper; almost as if they were doing magic that was a little bit above their level that they weren't actually allowed to play with. Which, they were. And, they weren't.

Glee, Shimmer and Twinkle looked a little worried at this stern note of caution from Mirth. He didn't tell them what the consequence of interfering with the spell might be but they took his warning seriously and put their trust in him. They were also very excited so happy to agree to the rules.

First Shimmer nodded her head in agreement to Mirth's rules. Glee and Twinkle first looked at her then turned to Mirth and enthusiastically nodded too in their eagerness to get on with the mischief. Then they all said thank you and goodbye to the rainbow and set off as they flew down to Cuckoo Village.

Once they reached the village, the four fairies separated and each flew under the front door, down the chimney or through an open window of a different house and went in search of the still sleeping child they had chosen as they prepared to cast their mischievous spell.

## CHAPTER 5

# No School Today

There are things that villages sometimes need but don't have because they are too small. Some of these are: a hospital, a fire station, a police station or a school. In these cases, the villagers have to go to the nearest town.

Plumton was the nearest town to Cuckoo Village and was about five miles away (or 'half a horizon' as farmer Crabtree sometimes called it).

The People of Cuckoo Village thought that five miles, or half a horizon, was the perfect distance for Plumton. It's near enough to be easy to get to when they need something special, yet far enough away that the busy goings on in the town aren't a disturbance when they want peace and quiet, which was most of the time.

Even Plumton is considered to be small for a town, but that's the place that the Cuckoo Villagers would go to or call when they needed, as they did on this day, a doctor.

No one can remember anyone in the village ever needing a policeman or a fireman as Cuckoo Village was one of the most safe and peaceful places in the world.

The children in Cuckoo Village did of course go to school in Plumton every day except Saturday and Sunday. And each day, those in the village who had children would take turns to drive them all to and from school.

As there were only fields, hills and woods either side

of the quiet country road between Cuckoo Village and Plumton and almost never any other cars, the drive to school only took ten minutes. Some of the children wished that it took much longer and for different reasons.

The children who didn't like school never wanted to arrive, so they wished the drive could take twice as long going to school and no time at all to get home. Others enjoyed the drive through the countryside and loved to be surrounded by nature, so they wished the drive both to and from school could go on and on. Some loved school so wanted to get there quickly but loved seeing the countryside on the way home so didn't mind if it took longer to drive back.

Every day, the children's school drive took the exact same road, Pheasant Lane, to Plumton, so they came to know the countryside very well. They knew it so well that they could tell when even the slightest of changes had taken place from one day to the next and especially when the seasons began to change.

On some mornings, the night-time rain had caused the grass in the fields to be the deepest of greens. On other days, such as a cold winter morning, the frost left a magical sparkle on the grass, the stone walls and even the trees as far as the eye could see. Well, it was actually fairies who left the magical sparkle. They just happened to use frost to do it.

When the geese and ducks on the little pond by the old water mill just outside the village had chosen early that morning to set off on their long journey to fly to the warm south for the winter, the pond seemed empty and sad. Then in springtime, when they returned and were spotted back on the pond, people were happy, and it felt like the official arrival of spring.

On the days that it snowed came the most miraculous of all transformations. The landscape changed from greens and browns to the whitest of white, as crisp snow blanketed the whole area. This made the countryside surrounding Cuckoo Village look like one giant, never-ending Christmas cake. Some of the snow-covered fir trees here and there even looked like candles.

That particular morning was autumn, so there wouldn't be any chance of snow for quite some time.

The sun had risen and was already stretching out its golden rays as it warmed and dried out the ground soaked from the night's rain. As it did so, a mist was beginning to hover just a few feet over most of the lower parts of the countryside surrounding Cuckoo Village.

Up above, the glorious rainbow that had inspired Farmer Crabtree and Nuzzler earlier that morning was still arching across the sky directly over the village.

There were no children to enjoy the wonderful scene on their usual drive along the country lane from Cuckoo Village to Plumton though. It was indeed a school morning; however, the drive to school had been cancelled and all the children of Cuckoo Village were staying home until further notice and that was quite acceptable to some of the children.

## CHAPTER 6

# Mysterious Calls

Doctor Clayton was the senior doctor in Plumton. The doctor had only been in his surgery for ten minutes that morning and he was already taking his third phone call from a worried parent from Cuckoo Village.

The call was from Mrs Robinson concerning her son Oliver. She was unaware that other Cuckoo parents had also called him with a similar, strange story.

As with Mr Sangfroid and Mrs Vauxhall, the first two villagers who had called the doctor in a panic, Mrs Robinson was unwilling to actually describe the problem in any detail for fear that the doctor would think it was a joke. She just begged him to come as soon as possible.

Doctor Clayton did believe Mrs Robinson as well as the other parents who had called, and although all of them had been unwilling to describe the exact nature of the problem, he had asked them if the children were in pain or any discomfort. They had all replied that their children seemed to feel completely fine and that it was only their 'appearance' that caused alarm.

Sitting at his desk with the phone in one hand, the Doctor leaned his head to the right slightly and rested it on two fingers as this always helped him to think when there was something that puzzled him. As with the other parents, he asked Mrs Robinson if she would like to bring her child into his surgery as he had appointments there today that could only be cancelled in the case of an emergency.

Mrs Robinson gave the same reply that Mr Sangfroid and Mrs Vauxhall had when they had also called a few minutes earlier. They had all told him that they were very sorry, and they could not explain why, but would really, rather not come into town and would he please make an exception and come as quickly as possible to pay a house call.

Of course, Doctor Clayton said he would and was just about to set off when he received his fourth call from a concerned Cuckoo parent. Mr Saffron called about his daughter Chloe. Mr Saffron didn't sound as worried as the other parents, but then again, he was always an optimistic and cheerful chap even when there was a problem to deal with.

Despite being quite calm, Mr Saffron, like the other parents, had been reluctant to explain the exact reason why it was probably better if the doctor could visit the children rather than the other way around. By this time the Doctor was becoming both quite concerned and very curious.

He also felt there was something unusual or special about that day. He had felt it as soon as he woke up; even before he received the four very curious phone calls from the Cuckooers. It was a beautifully strange anticipation. It wasn't Christmas day or his birthday, but for some reason he felt even happier than usual that morning and he didn't know why; and now he was called away to see patients with a mysterious . . . condition.

Doctor Clayton knew all the families in Cuckoo Village well as he either saw them here in town when they needed a doctor, or he paid a visit to the village on occasions such as today.

As he had been taking care of people in Plumton and the surrounding villages for most of his long life, he had not only known all the children in Cuckoo Village since they were born, but had been a doctor long enough to also known most of their parents since they were children too.

The doctor knew that of the twelve houses, including the village shop, and also nearby Crabtree Farm, only four of the families had children still at home. The others either did not have children or their children had already grown up and moved away.

How curious then that of the four families with children, all of them had called and asked him to do a house call. And although most had more than one child, they had each only reported a problem with one of their children.

For a moment he wondered if it could be some kind of prank they were playing on him. The folks in Cuckoo Village were as serious about serious things as anyone should be, but they were also a joyful people and knew how to have fun when fun was called for. So, he tried to think of any 'non-medical' reason the villagers might want to get him to Cuckoo Village.

He knew it wasn't April fool's day. It wasn't even April; it was late September. He didn't have an anniversary of any kind and it wasn't his birthday so there was no chance of it being a surprise celebration. Besides, the villagers knew his patients in Plumton had appointments that morning and he would have to ask some of the other doctors to see them. Some of his patients wouldn't be happy about that as they had been seeing Doctor Clayton all their lives and liked him very much as their doctor and always complained when he wasn't available. So, he knew the Cuckoo parents wouldn't play a joke that might cause others such an inconvenience.

The doctor decided that it definitely wasn't a prank, and that something was happening to the children of Cuckoo Village. But what could it be he wondered. He decided that, as they Cuckoo parents were not willing to tell him over the phone, the only way to find out was to pay some house calls and see for himself.

He asked the surgery's kindly receptionist Mrs Pindar to give his apology and reschedule his patients with other doctors and he asked Nurse Walton, to accompany him to Cuckoo Village.

When Nurse Walton asked about the reason they were being called out, to her surprise, he replied that he didn't really know. So, a curious Doctor Clayton and Nurse Walton set off for Cuckoo Village.

## CHAPTER 7

# A Drive in the Country

Despite feeling a little worried about what they might find in Cuckoo Village, Doctor Clayton couldn't help enjoying the autumn countryside as he and Nurse Walton drove along in his old-fashioned but very well cared for, green Morris Minor Traveller.

He had bought the Morris Minor Traveller when he was a young doctor in Plumton many, many years ago. It was a beauty then and it was still a beauty now as he always took good care to keep it polished and shiny and running well.

He was due to retire at the end of the year after a very long career as a doctor. That meant he'd had the dear little car for a great many years. It wasn't as old as his tongue, or even his teeth, but it was still quite old.

He had chosen the Morris Minor Traveller model as it had lots of space in the back and at a pinch, a patient could lay down with the back seats folded down if they needed to be taken to hospital. He also, love, love, loved that the car actually had a wooden frame made from English ash holding it together at the back. The idea of a part wooden car made him feel very happy for some reason and that had never changed. In fact, whenever he went for a drive, he would first give the wooden frame of his car a pat and say something like 'come on old girl'. Or if he arrived at his destination without breaking down, he would pat the wooden frame and say 'good girl'.

When the old car did break down (which was more often these days), he didn't think it was time to get rid of it and buy a new car as many people did. Instead, he thought of all the times it had looked after him and taken him and his family and his patients where he needed to go and all the happy times he had with the car. So, he only wanted to fix it and make it better, almost as if it were a patient.

Now that he'd fixed and driven the car so many times and so many miles over the years, it felt so much a part of his life that he looked on it as almost being a family member or favourite pet.

Behind the back seat was a light brown, wicker picnic basket. On top of the basket lay an old red, blue and green tartan blanket which he always sat on when enjoying a picnic.

The tartan picnic blanket would sometimes catch his eye as it got into the car and he would smile as he remembered a particularly enjoyable picnic he'd been on recently. Or looked forward to the next time he would get a chance to go on one. Apart from helping people and making them better, having a nice picnic was the thing Doctor Clayton enjoyed most in the whole world.

With Nurse Walton in the passenger seat beside him and his little black doctors' bag on the back seat, they had soon driven through the five miles of beautiful countryside which separated Cuckoo Village from Plumton. After passing the old water mill and the turn off to Crabtree farm, the little Morris Minor Traveller

chugged over a small hill and the village came into view.

It was indeed a tiny village at only twelve houses, and might not be noticed at all if the road didn't pass right through the middle of it with the houses on either side.

Farmer Crabtree would disagree, but for anyone else it was still early in the day. Doctor Clayton looked at his watch which, like his car, he'd had for a very long time. It had been a present from his proud younger sister from when he had first become a doctor. The watch told him that it was almost 9 am.

There was a low mist in the fields on either side of the road as the sun had dried what was left of the night's rain. This gave them the feeling that they were driving on the clouds.

As the old car took them towards the village, Doctor Clayton thought he could see a fading rainbow directly overhead. 'Nothing shy about that Rainbow. It must have been a beauty' he thought. Then turning to Nurse Walton, he smiled and said, "welcome to my favourite place in the whole world."

As they entered the village, the road started to curve and twist as it passed between the houses. The people who built the houses of Cuckoo Village hundreds of years ago had inconsiderately failed to take into account that one day people would invent cars and want to drive between the houses rather than ride a horse. The villagers liked the curvy road though because it caused cars to slow down when they passed through. This made it safer for the children of the village and quieter for everyone. The Cuckooers thought slowing down was good for the drivers too as they got to enjoy the beauty of their little

village for longer.

The first thing that came into view as they approached from the east was a sign which proudly declared 'CUCKOO VILLAGE'. After that nurse Walton cooed as they passed a pretty, old house with a thatched roof. She told Doctor Clayton it was so quaint with the thick straw for a roof instead of the usual tiles.

The next few houses in the village were very close to the road on either side. Their front doors, of all different colours and shapes, opened onto the pavement. Then the road twisted some more and the houses which followed had little front gardens with low hedges or fences around them.

Doctor Clayton parked the Morris Minor in the middle of the village just before a grassy turn off to the right. The turn off wasn't exactly a road, it was more a dirt path that led up to a house which was set further back that the others and was a little bigger than the rest of the houses in the Village.

The house that the doctor had parked along-side was in fact the Evans' shop, and nurse Walton looked a little confused when she saw the funny hand painted sign above the shop entrance. The sign read 'QUARNER SHOP'.

"Quarner Shop?" she read aloud in a puzzled tone.

The doctor smiled, "Mr Evans is quite a character. In nearby towns, the shop is well known to people for Mrs Crabtree's Crabtree Farm Famous Butter."

"But why Quarner Shop?" asked Nurse Walton.

CHAPTER 8

# The Quarner Shop

Doctor Clayton smiled as he always enjoyed telling the story of how the Quarner Shop got its name.

“One day Mr Evans took umbridge when a customer from Plumton said ‘it wasn’t really a shop as it’s so tiny so it’s only half a shop, and as it’s only open part time that makes it just a quarter of a shop’.”

Doctor Clayton continued “Mr Evans had argued that, ‘any place people sell things and other people buy things is a shop’. The customer laughed and said 'It's a Cuckoo village all right'. . . By the next morning Mr Evans had the sign up, a quarter shop on a corner so; Quarner Shop!”

Nurse Walton gave an amused sniff at this, which is more than Mrs Evans had done. Every chance she got, in the month after her husband had put up the sign, she had complained to whoever in the village would listen about what a crackpot her husband was.

‘Him and his ways’ she would grumble, though with a glint in her eyes that showed she actually looked forward to his next stunt.

Mr Evans had spent the entire month with a fierce and triumphant ‘Fixed you, so I did’ look on his face. It was a look that told anyone who cared to bring the subject up that they were now stating the obvious. After all, signs are not to be argued or agreed with. They just state what is. A quarter shop and a corner shop then, subject closed.

CHAPTER 9

# Mr Evan's Eyebrow

As the doctor and Nurse Walton got out of the car, they noticed Mr Evans at the door of the Quarner Shop peering through the glass just above the 'OPEN' sign. It was a few minutes after 9 am and he was getting ready to close.

The shop usually opened for a few hours in the morning and then again in the late afternoon/early evening. Mr and Mrs Evans were actually retired but they opened the shop twice a day because there wasn't another shop for miles, and they liked taking care of the community. And it also gave them a chance to regularly interact with Cuckoo villagers, who were their favourite people in the whole world.

Instead of closing up though, Mr Evans came out to greet them.

"Hallo doctor. Out on a call are ya?" he asked.

"How are things Mr Evans?" Doctor Clayton greeted him back.

Even though all the people in Cuckoo Village were Doctor Clayton's patients as well as his friends, he never used the adult's first names when he was on an official call. Not because he wasn't friendly with them; he was, very. He had been brought up to show respect to people and this was his way of doing so.

Mr Evans eyed the little black doctor's bag that Doctor Clayton was pulling from the back seat of the

Morris Minor. He wasn't usually so nosey about the doctor's business, so his obvious curiosity made Doctor Clayton wonder what he knew about the mysterious phone calls that had brought him to the Village.

As Mr Evans seemed to be gearing up to push for more information, he tried to head him off by introducing Nurse Walton. It was her first visit to Cuckoo Village, and he'd brought her along as much to introduce her to everyone as to assist in whatever treatment might be needed for the children.

"Mr Evans, this is Nurse Walton, it's her first time in the village."

"I know that doctor. Isn't much appens ere as scapes me. Or don't, as the case may be. It's very nice to meet you Nurse Walton and welcome to Cuckoo Village" he said as he gave her entire arm good shake.

"Nice to meet you too Mr Evans" replied Nurse Walton as she rescued her arm.

He then skilfully moved the conversation back onto the subject of the doctor's visit.

"F'rinstance, we usually gets at least a couple ah the little un's duckin in ere afore they make the school run. Should'a stayed in bed this mornin though. There's not been a soul about. Not one car pass by either cept your old lass". Anyone'd think t'were Christmas day."

Doctor Clayton knew this was Mr Evans' invitation for the doctor to tell him what was going on, but they both knew a doctor never talks about his patients to others so he just smiled and shrugged his shoulders.

"We'll see" said the doctor.

Mr Evans could see that the doctor was in a serious mood despite his friendly smile, so he let him off easily .

. . for now. He then changed the subject.

"Oh well, p'raps it's something to do with all that rain we ad through the night. Not exactly shepherds delight was it? Me and Mrs Evans arf expected to see Noah floating by come mornin".

As the doctor smiled at Mr Evans last point, Nurse Walton sneaked past them both and headed for the shop doorway as the 'open' sign was still facing out.

"I'm just going to pop in for a minute doctor," she informed him without waiting for a reply.

As she did so, Mr Evans' bushy right eyebrow lifted and followed her around, with his right eye and the rest of his head in tow. The eyebrow was checking for the slightest clue that Nurse Walton might find the shop 'unusual' in any way.

All seemed well as the eyebrow didn't detect anything untoward at all in Nurse Walton's attitude about the shop. Not a sniff, a furrowed brow or even questioning look. Until with a 'ding' she had disappeared inside.

Satisfied that the Quarner Shop had been respected, the eyebrow then returned to its usual position and resumed its normal duties of keeping the sweat from Mr Evans' right eye and generally matching his other eyebrow.

Nurse Walton had passed a very important test and was now fully welcome in Cuckoo Village as far as Mr Evans and his eyebrow were concerned.

"Well now, the old lass is still taking good care of you eh?" Mr Evans nodded with affection at the doctor's car again.

"Oh yes, I think she'll go for about as long as I will," answered the doctor with pride.

## CHAPTER 10

# A Treasure Cave

As the doctor and Mr Evans continued chatting outside, Nurse Walton stepped into the Quarner Shop and then marched up to the counter. It wasn't much of a march though as just one step achieved both actions of stepping into the shop and up to the counter.

The inside of the shop was tiny. It could have been the small living room of any house if you took away the cabinets of sweets and various tinned food and replaced them with a couch and armchair. Whatever its size or times of opening though, it fully qualified as a shop to Nurse Walton because it had the one thing that all truly great little sweet shops havc: atmosphere.

The little Quarner Shop had fresh, sweet-smelling air and a warm, golden glow. Nurse Walton wasn’t sure where it came from exactly and it was the same in the local sweet shop near to the house she had grown up in. All the best little shops seemed to have a warm golden glow about them.

The interior of the little shop reminded Nurse Walton of when she was a child and, as she drew closer to such shops, how the inviting warmth would pour out of the windows and doorway and spill onto the street like honey made of light.

It was most magical to little Jenny Walton in the frosty, dark, late afternoon winters when her mother would have her wrapped up tight in her coat, hat, scarf and gloves.

She would step out of the cold and into her local shop and feel its warmth on her face and would be surrounded by sweets of every shape, colour and most importantly taste that she could possibly imagine.

This is why the fresh, sweet fragrance in the Cuckoo Village Quarner Shop caused Nurse Walton to think back to when she was a child. It wasn't really thinking though, it was more like feeling. Some memories, especially childhood ones, come back through the heart rather than the head and are often suddenly triggered by lovely and familiar smells.

Nurse Walton turned from the counter to look at the rows of sweet jars. She remembered that as a child on the short wintery walk to and from school, she would be wrapped up so tight in her hooded duffle coat that she couldn't easily turn her head. She would have to walk around her local sweet shop swivelling her entire body left and right to look around and lean back and forward to look up and down until she found the object of her desire.

Now that she had children of her own, she loved to watch as they did the same thing. Sometimes though, she liked to pretend she was still a child herself when she stepped inside such a lovely shop. She would know what she wanted as her favourites were set by now, but she would still make herself wait as long as possible before making a purchase. It was as if she couldn't bear to bring the joy of selection to an end by making the final choice.

Alone in the delightful little Quarner Shop, Nurse Walton closed her eyes and, lifting her head slightly, she sniffed in slowly and lightly. When she opened her eyes again, a little old lady with a cup of tea warming her hands had quietly appeared and was standing on the other side of the counter. Nurse Walton suddenly felt embarrassed and couldn't think of anything to say or what to ask for.

"Erm, I'm here with the doctor," she said as if it were an excuse for something.

"Why, am I sick?" chuckled the lady. She then took a sip tea with her smiling eyes twinkling over the rim of the cup.

The lady was old, but the wrinkles that appeared around her eyes as she smiled were beautiful; like rays of sunshine spreading out from a warm heart.

Nurse Walton's father had once said '*It's not a matter of being 'young or old' but rather 'fresh or stale'. The secret to getting older is to be mature but also fresh.*' Nurse Walton felt the wisdom of her father's words when she looked at the little old lady in the shop. The feeling that came from her was like a fresh fragrance but not an actual smell, just a light and kindly feeling. Nurse Walton imagined that this was what Mrs Santa Clause would be like.

"No, er," Nurse Walton still felt embarrassed over the 'sniffing in' but found that the lady's smile and sing song eyes were so kindly that she didn't mind being embarrassed. So she just chuckled herself.

Now that the teacup was back to warming the lady's hands, Nurse Walton could see the kindly look on the whole of her face. It was one of those faces that were still beautiful even in old age.

"I suppose you've met Mr Evans out there, well I'm Mrs Evans. It's lovely to meet you dear," she greeted.

"Oh, I'm Nur. . er, Jenny, Jenny Walton. Pleased to meet you Mrs Evans," replied Nurse Walton feeling a little bit like a teenager again.

At this moment Mr Evans came back into the shop and Doctor Clayton popped his head through the door.

“Hello Mrs Evans, Mr Evans behaving himself, is he?”

“Hello doctor. He's no worse at least” came Mrs Evans sing-song reply.

She then gave Mr Evans a sideways glance while he skulked around and alongside her then stood his ground with the full authority of the counter in front of him.

“Ready nurse?” asked the doctor.

“Er, yes, just coming,” she replied as she stuck her hand into a clear jar and lifted as many flat lollipops of all colours from it as her fist could hold without getting trapped in the jar.

With the doctor waiting patiently, she really felt like a child again as Mrs Evans expertly counted the sweets and quickly and put them into a white paper bag then spun it round so the twist at the top would seal it.

“Twenty-five pence please love,” said Mrs Evans handing the bag of lollipops over as if it were a prize.

Nurse Walton paid for the lollipops and thanking Mrs Evans, left the shop with a "Nice to meet you" and then a "Sorry Doctor, sweet tooth."

“Good job I’m not your dentist,” said the doctor as they left the shop with the same ‘ding’ they had entered.

Nurse Walton smiled and put the lollipops into her bag without offering one to the doctor or taking one herself and followed him as he headed for the first house call of the day.

# CHAPTER 11

# The Robinson Family

The Robinson family had lived at number three, Cuckoo Village for as long as Doctor Clayton could remember, and the three children were the third generation of Robinsons that he had taken care of.

Like most of the houses in Cuckoo Village, the Robinson's was charming with its sandstone walls and quaint olde world front windows. It was also the first house on the east side of the village with a front garden. There waiting at the gate were an anxious looking Mr and Mrs Robinson.

'It must be something serious indeed if Mr Robinson hasn't gone into work yet' thought the doctor. Mr Robinson worked in Plumton as an architect and usually left for work at seven thirty sharp every morning.

"Mr and Mrs Robinson, good morning. This is Nurse Walton," the doctor said as they opened the gate for him and walked with him up their curvy garden path with Nurse Walton close behind.

"Hello" greeted Nurse Walton in a cheerful voice.

She was always cheerful and friendly with patients as she liked to encourage them even if they weren't feeling well or were worried about someone.

Doctor Clayton and Nurse Walton could see the worry on Mr & Mrs Robinson's faces, so they didn't mind when neither of them returned his or Nurse Walton's greeting and instead just quickly ushered them into the house.

"This way doctor, it's Oliver, I'm ever so worried" said Mrs Robinson as she held her own hand for comfort.

"He, he seems alright, no temperature or pain but he looks, erm unusual" said Mr Robinson with an almost embarrassed look on his face.

"I see. In bed is he?" asked the doctor as he moved towards the stairs.

"Um, no actually, he's in the kitchen having breakfast."

"Oh" replied the doctor feeling quite surprised to hear that Oliver wasn't in bed. People only call the doctor out when it is something serious and he didn't usually arrive to find his patients up and about and having a meal.

Seeing the surprise on Doctor Claytons' face, Mr Robinson said apologetically, "we offered to take it up to him, but he wanted to eat with his brothers."

Then, in the kind of loving but long-suffering tone, he added "he gets quite . . . agitated when he thinks the others are getting something he isn't."

"Indeed" nodded the doctor. He remembered how they had once brought Oliver into Plumton to see him for treatment for a small burn on his finger. Mr & Mrs Robinson had lit the candles on a birthday cake for his older brother David and had let his younger brother Jonathan blow out the match. Oliver had sulked that he wanted to blow it out and had insisted that his mother light another one just so he could do so. Mrs Robinson had told him not to sulk, and Oliver had snatched the box of kitchen matches and tried to strike one himself but had burned his finger a little as the match lit up.

Doctor Clayton knew that, although most times being a well-behaved boy, Oliver was a handful of trouble whenever he even suspected he might be missing out.

Raising his eyebrows, the doctor turned to the living room door and began to open it as he remembered from previous visits that the living room opened up to the kitchen at the back of the house.

At this, Mr Robinson put out his hand to gently stop the doctor for a moment, so he paused with the door open just a little.

Mrs Robinson sighed strangely. The sigh sounded like she was forcing it out and trying to hold it in at the same time.

"Doctor, you . . . might want to prepare yourself. This isn't anything . . . normal."

Nurse Walton stood bemused further back in the hall by the front door as she looked from the Robinsons to the doctor then back again. They had been eager to get them in the house but now seemed to have trouble letting them get any further than the front hall. She got the feeling that they were embarrassed to have them seen outside at their door but just as embarrassed for them to actually see little Oliver.

"Not normal? Illness never is. But, come now, I'm sure we can take care of him" answered the doctor encouragingly.

He then moved to enter the living room one more time only for Mrs Robinson to motion for him not to enter quite yet.

Mrs Robinson's reluctance to let him see Oliver was making him even more curious. What kind of illness could be so embarrassing to the parents he wondered? He had been a doctor for almost fifty years and had seen everything, or so he thought. But, it seemed, there was always room for surprise in life.

"Ahhmmm . . . he's green" Mrs Robinson suddenly blurted out not knowing how else to say it.

"Green?" answered the doctor, now wondering what little Oliver had eaten to make him so.

"I mean . . . GREEEEEEN" repeated Mrs Robinson in a deeper voice than usual and leaning in a little with her eyes widened as she said it. Then she continued, "green face, green hair, green eyes, green teeth and even his fingernails are green."

"Oh" replied the doctor.

"Even stranger, as if it were possible, his pyjamas! Last night? Blue. This morning? Green. It's like . . . something has dyed him green all over while he slept" added Mr Robinson with a bonkers look on his face.

Doctor Clayton listened to this in a kind of amused disbelief. He was ready for something unusual, but this was just plain weird. The doctor wondered if it was Mr and Mrs Robinson who were unwell. He had read of a brain problem once that caused a man in Argentina to see everything in only black and white . . . but not green. Besides, Mr and Mrs Robinson couldn't both have the same problem with sight. Also, they didn't seem to see anyone else as being green, only Oliver. He decided that the only thing for it was to see for himself.

"I'd better take a look. Come on nurse," he said as he reached again for the door in the kind of determined way that showed his mind was made up and he wouldn't be deterred a third time.

Mr and Mrs Robinson said nothing more. Now that the doctor had been warned; all they could do was let him pass and see for himself.

## CHAPTER 12

# Shenanigans

Earlier that morning, Mirth, had arrived at the Robinson home to cast his naughty spell. He had done this by knocking three times on the still sleeping Oliver's forehead like it was a door. Then he spent the morning with Oliver's two brothers enjoying the scene of little Oliver waking up to find himself totally, completely green.

Mirth was also on the lookout for any opportunity to cause just a little bit more mischief.

While the doctor waited in the hallway listening to Mr & Mrs Robinson's cautions about what he and Nurse Walton were about to see, Mirth hovered, unseen above the three Robinson children.

The three brothers were sitting around the kitchen table at the back of the house. They had finished breakfast and were chatting and playing. Two of the three Robinson children were in an especially good mood as they had the day off school.

Oliver's older brother David, and his younger brother Jonathan didn't seem to be as worried as their parents by the fact that one of them had woken up to find himself transformed into a totally, completely green eight-year-old. To them it was no stranger than if Oliver woken up covered in pink spots, which, in fact, he had just last year when he had the measles. If anything, to Oliver's annoyance, they found his current condition to be quite amusing.

Jonathan, who at seven years old was the youngest, was standing on one leg leaning on the kitchen table drawing a picture of Oliver with his crayons.

Mirth flew down and settled on Jonathan’s right shoulder to admire the picture which was a box which represented the house, two stick figure adults, two children and a green smudge with even darker green spots for eyes which Mirth guessed was Oliver.

Oliver was also looking at the picture and wasn't happy about it at all. He was even less happy that Jonathan kept looking up at Oliver while grinning to make sure he was drawing an accurate green smudge.

"Why don't you just take a photo?" Oliver pouted in sarcastic complaint at his younger brother’s amused gaze.

Mirth quickly whispered into Jonathan's ear, then Jonathan said, "good idea". Then taking a few steps into the living room he picked up the family camera and took a photograph of his own drawing.

"Ha ha, very funny" said Oliver, who wasn't in the mood for jokes.

Mirth flew over to David who at age eleven was the eldest. Although David was the leader of the three, he was also the naughtiest and loved making trouble and that was one of the many things that Mirth liked about him.

When he had woken up and first saw that his little brother was totally, completely green, he thought Christmas and his birthday had both come early and on the same day. He couldn't believe how great it was and had excitedly called to his parents, not in alarm but as if he'd just found some treasure.

Mirth liked David very much. He was a troublemaker just like himself but never in a cruel way. David was a kind older brother most of the time, but he always made time for mischief. Mirth flew very close to David's right ear and began to whisper into it.

David couldn't hear Mirth of course, just as he couldn't see him, but he got Mirth's suggestion as if it was his own idea. His eyes went wide for a moment then they suddenly became narrow as he looked to the right without moving his head. He also bit his lower lip and took on a naughty smile.

"I've just had a great idea Johnny" said David as if it were something that was going to benefit Jonathan. Then "Gimme your face painting stuff."

"Why" asked Jonathan.

"Because I said so" came the only answer an older, and more importantly bigger brother needs.

"All right, but be careful, it's very messy you know" answered Jonathan in a pretend serious voice as if he were a long-suffering parent instead of the youngest brother who gets pushed around a lot.

"Sit here Johnny, I'm gonna paint your face green to play a trick on them" explained David. He then grabbed his little brother by the scruff of his collar and pulled him down onto a chair without waiting for him to do as he was told. He was in a hurry as he had heard his parents go into the garden when the doctor's car arrived in the village.

"What, nooooo!" exclaimed Jonathan straining to get away like an agitated puppy tied up by its leash.

David pulled him down again. "DO IT" he urged.

"I don't want to" whined Jonathan in submission as he

flopped into the chair in protest. He knew he would have to obey as David was using his 'it's already decided' voice.

"Do it, or I won't let you play out with us anymore" threatened David. He didn't wait for a reply; he just quickly got to work daubing green face paint on Jonathan's scrunched up, unhappy face.

Mirth was happy to see that David was smart enough not to use felt pens or other kinds as they would be poisonous if you draw on the skin a lot. He knew that face paint was specially made for that purpose so was safe. He was happy to see that David was his kind of mischief maker. Naughty, but in a sensible way.

Being the youngest, Jonathan usually suffered from the ancient tradition of seniority when it came to power struggles among him and his two elder brothers. David sometimes pushed Oliver or Jonathan around, Oliver pushed Jonathan around and Jonathan had no one to do the same to. They didn't even have a dog that he could order around; even though he had begged his parents for one. The only power he had lay in his very well practiced and often used baby voice. Some people use a baby voice to get nice things that they want, but Jonathan used it to control two giant robots and make them attack David and Oliver.

He had learned at an early age that parents were sometimes like puppets. Instead of being controlled by strings though, they could be controlled by a whiny baby voice; especially if it came from their youngest child.

Jonathan decided not to use the giant robots this time though as not being able to play out with his brothers was too high a price to pay for victory. So, he just sat there as

David dabbed more green paint over his face, hands and even his hair.

'Now I'll never get a dog' he thought sullenly.

Mirth hovered around them excitedly, pleased with the way things were going. Every now and then he whispered into David's ear 'you missed a spot' or 'a little more there'. He wished his friends were here to see this little bit of extra mischief. He knew it would make a great story to tell later though. Hearing about something wonderful that happened to someone you love is the next best thing to sharing the moment with them. Sometimes, only sometimes, it's almost as good to tell people about a special moment as actually sharing the moment with them.

Mirth already looked forwards to reuniting later with Glee, Shimmer and Twinkle so he could tell them about what he got up to with these three funny little boys.

Oliver started to enjoy himself and looked very pleased with the proceedings. He was glad to have the attention off himself for a while, and also glad that someone in the room was less happy than he was.

Oliver didn't just dislike it when others had something good that he didn't have, he also disliked it when others didn't have something bad that he had. As selfish as he was with his blessings, he was more than generous with his misfortune. So, he just sat there with a slice of half-eaten toast in his hand as he made the same narrow eyed, lower lip biting face as his mischievous, instigator brother David.

"Yeah, make him stand there" Oliver said, pointing at the centre of the living room with his toast as if it was a magician's wand. Mirth found this action to be quite funny and was also glad to see poor little Oliver's spirits lifted as he was enjoying the mischief within mischief.

"Finished!" declared David in a hurry as he stood Jonathan up and pushed him backwards a few steps so that he could admire his own handy work. Then, after quickly leaning in a few times and adding more dabs, he was satisfied with the green face painting job he'd done and gave Jonathan his marching orders.

"Just stand there and look at them when they come in but don't say anything . . . or else" David commanded as he dragged Jonathan off the chair by the same collar he had tugged to sit him down. Then, he turned to Oliver who was getting increasingly excited and waving his half slice of toast around like a victory flag.

"Ollie, move over there around the corner so they don't see you when they come in."

“I want to see” complained Oliver.

“Then they will see you and it will spoil it. Go on” answered David strictly.

Oliver sulked over to the kitchen and just about hid himself out of view.

When David had orchestrated the mischief to Mirth's satisfaction, Mirth whispered again in David's ear to let him know that everything was fine. David felt pleased at the set up and sat back down at the kitchen table where he could get a good view of the ambush. Mirth did the same by flying up and sitting on a picture frame that hung on the living room wall. He was excited to see the doctor's face when he saw the badly painted, unmagically green Jonathan.

Mirth had known what was in David's heart. After all, a fairy can achieve much more when it whispers into a human's ear if the human is already thinking or feeling along the lines of what the fairy is suggesting. That's why Mirth would always say 'a nudge is better than a shove' when he was teaching his friends how to influence humans.

David was certainly a naughty and mischievous older brother and often got Oliver and Jonathan into trouble with his antics. But he also cared about his younger brothers and always protected and encouraged them when they really needed it.

Mirth knew that despite David teasing Oliver, he also had sympathy for him and was happy to create a scene with the face painted Jonathan because he knew it would cheer Oliver up and also distract him from the fact that had woken up as green as a grape.

Oliver was going to learn something today, that was part of the magic of the mischief. Mirth could feel it and was excited about that, but he also knew that some lessons can be painful ones and he wanted to make this as much fun as possible for everyone.

Jonathan wasn't as happy as his brothers at that moment. He did as he was told though and sheepishly stood in the centre of the living room waiting to shock the doctor and embarrass his parents. He expected them to pretend to smile and tell him off in a gentle way, but to shout a bit more loudly when the guests had left.

He had his defence already prepared though. It wasn't hard to remember as it was always the same. The magic words 'they made me do it' usually got him out of most trouble he was in; even when it wasn't exactly true sometimes.

His two silly, older brothers hadn't quite figured out

that the not so magical words 'no we didn't' didn't work so well; but they always tried to use them.

Oliver had stopped waving his toast around and was getting a bit upset because David had moved him to a place in the kitchen even further around the corner and sat him on a stool where the doctor wouldn't see him. This also meant that he wouldn't be able to see the doctor. He started to get antsy at the thought of his two brothers enjoying the adult’s reaction without him. Oliver leaned so far to his right to get a better view that he almost fell off his stool.

"Get back Ollie, they'll see you" ordered David.

"It's not fair, you can see them, but I won't be able to. I wanna see them too."

"Well you can't cause it'll spoil it so sit still" came David's final firm reply. Then suddenly "they're coming".

# CHAPTER 13

# In Big Trouble

Doctor Clayton stepped into the Robinsons' living room with an open mind. On the one hand, he had lived and worked as a doctor for a very long time and had seen just about every kind of illness there is but was always ready to be surprised and see something new. On the other hand, Mr and Mrs Robinson had told him that their son Oliver was green. Not just feeling ill, eaten far too many sweets green . . . but green face, teeth, eyes hair and even green fingernails 'and' pyjamas? Even with an open mind, this sounded too strange to possibly be true. Well, now it was time to see for himself.

What the doctor saw shocked him, made him want to laugh out loud and also feel a little bit angry all at the same time. He half expected to see TV cameras as a great trick was being played on him. But no, there were no cameras, just a messily painted, bashful looking green boy standing before him in the middle of the room.

Now Doctor Clayton really couldn't believe what he was seeing. Would Mr and Mrs Robinson really have him cancel his appointments and come all the way here just for a joke? He knew them to be people of very good character and doing so was far less likely in his mind than even a boy waking up one morning totally, completely green. Anyway, they surely weren't that good at acting as they seemed truly worried just a moment ago when they were warning him what to expect when he saw Oliver.

So not knowing what to think or do, he just stared wide eyed at the roughly painted green boy before him. Then, after a moment, the doctor turned to the parents for an explanation.

Nurse Walton was just as surprised as Doctor Clayton but couldn't help herself from letting out a short laugh before she got control of herself and assumed a serious face again.

Mr and Mrs Robinson looked even more shocked than the doctor and knowing their children better than their children even knew themselves, they correctly guessed not only how the trick had been played but also who the culprit was.

"David Robinson, look what you've done to Jonathan. This is serious you know, and the doctor doesn't have time for your shenanigans!" complained Mrs Robinson feeling both anger and embarrassment.

"Tttshhhh, shenanigans" sniggered Oliver as he peeked his truly green face around the corner to get a look at the shocked adults.

Oliver always laughed when his mother used the word shenanigans. Especially when they were in front of others. Mr Robinson sometimes joked that their mother thought this made her sound posh, so they all usually teased her whenever she said it.

Nurse Walton's had guessed exactly what shenanigans were being perpetrated as soon as she saw the green face-painted boy. It's just the kind of thing that her older brothers got up to when she was a child; usually with her playing the unwilling role of the unfortunate Jonathan.

"Jonathan Robinson go upstairs and wash that off right now" snapped Mrs Robinson.

Jonathan didn't need telling twice. He quickly weaved himself between the four adults and headed for the living room door. He cringed as he passed the two giant robots whose attack stare was on him for a change.

'Aw, they won't be handing out puppies anytime in the near future that's for sure' he thought.

At first, David looked like he was crying but he wasn't; he was laughing. He knew he was in trouble but thought that laughing out loud would get him a worse punishment. So, he tried unsuccessfully to hide his laughter.

With his head in his hands and his elbows on his knees, he was bending forwards biting his bottom lip to make it hurt in the hope that it would stop him from laughing out loud. He also looked down and to the right in a desperate effort to hide his face and stop any sound from escaping as his chest heaved and convulsed.

On the back of these efforts, David also had the totally unrealistic hope that he might be able to deny that he had anything to do with it - but if they saw him laughing that wouldn't work.

Unfortunately, the more effort he put into not laughing the funnier the situation seemed. He tried his hardest not to look at his parents or the doctor as he knew he would lose what little control over himself he had if he did.

The harder the lad tried not to look at them the more he felt compelled to do so. It didn't help that a giggling Mirth had flown down to him and whispered "look, look, look!" in his ear before flying back up and settling on a picture frame to survey the hilarious goings on.

Eventually, David lost the battle and couldn't stop himself from looking at their shocked faces. As soon as he saw them, great gulps of laughter started to leak from him, and he began dribbling like a baby.

His laughing became so painful that for a moment he thought he was going pass out. He bit his lip even harder to distract himself from how funny the look on all the adult's faces were, but it didn't work. Then he realised that bending over and hiding his face when he had already started laughing out loud was pointless. So he let go and sat up as he laughed hysterically while pointing at them as if this communicated some sort of explanation.

Luckly for David, the Doctor Clayton and the lady had already caught sight of the truly, totally, completely green Oliver and were too astonished to be angry with him at that moment. So he continued to laugh his head off as he covered his belly with his left arm and continued pointing in their general direction with his right.

As he moved his hands away from his face, strands of snot stretched out like he was pulling chewing gum between his fingers and teeth. Even though he was disgusted with that himself, he couldn't do anything about it for the moment because he was still laughing so hard.

Mirth was laughing just as hard as David was. He was laughing so hard that he had fallen off the picture frame. He was laughing almost as much at the sight of David's desperate attempt to hide his own laughter as he was at the adult's shock and embarrassment. Then he laughed even more at the disgusting sight of David look of disgust at his own snot covered hands.

Mirth's uncontrollable laughter meant that although he had fallen off the picture frame, he couldn't concentrate on flying no matter how much he tried. As a result, he started to slide slowly down the wall and onto the mantelpiece above the fireplace.

For a while he just lay there on his belly kicking his feet and banging his right fist down again and again while pointing in the general direction of first the doctor then David then back to his parents.

Then Mirth became more excited when he noticed just how much snot was goo-ing between David's hands and face.

"SNOT!!! . . . we have snot" declared Mirth in a triumphant shout - even though no one could hear him.

"Haaaar, Glee will never beat that."

Dispite Mirth's seniority in the group, Mirth and Glee were still quite young fairies, and just like some young humans, they thought gooey, sticky, snotty, things were funny; but only when they were on 'others' of course.

They were always challenging each other at something and earlier in the day Glee had bet Mirth that he could get more snot out of his child than the others could. Mirth had enthusiastically accepted the challenge, but the girls had refused to join in the bet and told the boys that they were disgusting, which made the boys very happy.

As Oliver had already shown his truly green face, there was no reason for him to stay hidden. He stepped out and looked at everyone as if he'd just arrived and knew nothing of the trick his brother had played on them.

After having thoroughly enjoyed the trick, he was now so busy trying to look innocent that he quite forgot how unusual his own appearance was.

The doctor looked at Oliver as if an alien had just

landed; he even had his head tilted to one side a little. Oliver didn't know much about medicine, but he guessed that it wasn't a good sign if a doctor tilted his head to one side when he looked at you.

"THIS . . . is Oliver, doctor" said Mrs Robinson almost as an apology for the mix up.

“He's grown a little since you last saw him" added Mr Robinson.

Nurse Walton kept the exact same expression of frozen surprise with her hand over her mouth as she stared at Oliver.

“Oh . . . my!” she exclaimed.

## CHAPTER 14

# The Real Oliver

"Well, he certainly is green!" agreed the doctor as he continued to stare at the greenest and in fact only green boy he had ever seen; along with his green hair, teeth, nails and even pyjamas. Then shaking himself out of the shock of seeing a real green boy, he said "Okay, let's have a look at you lad."

Doctor Clayton sat Oliver on the living room couch, then putting his doctor's bag down, sat beside him. In the bag, he had all the things a doctor needs. He had a stethoscope for listening to a patient's heartbeat and breathing. A thermometer for checking a patient's temperature. A reflex hammer for tapping a patient below the knee to see if their leg gives a kick. A tongue depressor which looked like an ice lolly stick and is used for holding the patients' tongue down so they can see their throat. He even had a magnifying glass. Although that is something most doctors don’t usually carry but he had occasionally found it useful over the years.

He checked all the things a doctor usually checks when they have no idea what might be causing a problem. After telling Oliver to breathe in and out deeply and listening to his chest with his stethoscope, he put a very dry lollipop stick into his mouth to hold down his tongue then told him to say 'aaaahh' while he shone a light into his mouth to see if everything was fine.

Oliver was amused by the attention and obeyed the

doctor's instructions as he said “ahhhhhhhh” for much longer than was needed.

The doctor checked Oliver's green eyes, his green ears, his green nose and just about everything else that he could think of which also happened to be green, and everything seemed normal . . . apart from the patient being totally, completely green.

He put a glass thermometer under Oliver's tongue and told him to keep it there. Oliver always had the urge to crunch down on them so had to concentrate hard to stop himself. After a moment the doctor removed the thermometer and hmm'ed that the lad's temperature was fine.

Apart from the fact that the Oliver was totally, completely green, there seemed to be nothing wrong with him at all. It was as if someone had simply dipped him in green paint while he had been sleeping but for once, David wasn't a suspect because he clearly wasn't that good at painting children.

The Doctor completed his examination of Oliver then stood up and stepped back to look at him from a distance. First folding his arms, then tipping his head to the right slightly again, he slowly raised his right hand and placed the first two fingers against his temple to support his tilted head. He then took a long, ponderous breath in through his nose, held it for a moment and then breathed out through pursed lips in a sudden, soft burst of air.

He did this whenever he was struggling to find the answer to some difficult puzzle as it helped him to concentrate.

With anyone else this wouldn't look so strange, but he also had the habit of sticking out his thumb and along with the two fingers he was resting his head on while deep in thought, this had the unfortunate effect of making it look like he was pretending to shoot himself in the head.

This was especially worrying for some of his patients to see. Most just found it funny though and trying not to laugh helped not to worry too much about their illness.

The only one who didn't notice was the Doctor himself, and no one had ever had the courage to tell him how silly he looked. He sometimes wondered why some of his patients suddenly smiled though.

Everyone in the room, apart from David, smiled at this sight and Oliver actually giggled. David was still sitting at the kitchen table and was on the doctor's left side so couldn't see how funny the doctor looked with two fingers pressed against the right side of his head and his thumb stuck out.

David frowned and wondered why everyone had suddenly smiled. For a moment he wondered if a great trick had been played on the master trickster himself. In fact, it had, as Mirth was the real master trickster (according to Mirth himself), just David didn't know it and the doctor making everyone smile was only a small part of the trick Mirth was playing on everyone that day.

Doctor Clayton stopped shooting himself in the head and reaching for his medical bag, he started putting away all the things he had used for the examination.

"Well, without further tests I'm afraid I can't find anything amiss with young master Oliver. He seems to be as fit and healthy as any boy his age should be" the doctor concluded with a shake of his head.

"Should you perhaps take him back to Plumton with

you doctor?" asked Mr Robinson.

"Possibly, possibly yes" mused the doctor. Then "as it happens, yours is not the only call I have this morning. The other three families called me around about the same time you did, so why don't you keep little Ollie here for the moment while Nurse Walton and I check on them."

When Doctor Clayton said 'the other three families' Mr and Mrs Robinson knew exactly what he meant. Even though there were twelve homes in Cuckoo Village, only four of them had children.

"Goodness, do you think the other children are green too doctor?" asked Mrs Robinson now looking even more concerned and wondering if they caught it from Oliver or if Oliver caught it from them.

"I think today is shaping up to be one of those days when anything is possible Mrs Robinson" answered the doctor with a reassuring smile.

As they prepared to exit the living room, Nurse Walton gave David a quick, secret smile that said, 'I respect your work young man.' David grinned back sheepishly with pride.

She then dipped into her bag and produced some of the lollipops she had bought at Mr Evans' Quarner Shop and gave one to David and also to Jonathan who had reappeared with a half-washed face. She had one for Oliver but didn't give it to him yet as the doctor was looking him over one last time before they moved to the next house.

Oliver's green eyes became very wide, as he took in a short, sudden breath though flared nostrils and held in the breath while puffing out his chest.

"What about me? Don't I get one? I'm the one who's

funny?” he complained indignantly.

“Yessss Oliver, I’m sure you’ll get a lollipop” answered Mr Robinson.

Both David and Jonathan wasted no time and had already unwrapped their lollipop and were exaggerating how delicious they were to tease Oliver.

“Mmmmm” moaned David and Jonathan in unison.

“Of course, here you are Oliver, what colour would you like” answered Nurse Walton as she fanned out several different coloured lollipops and held them out for him to choose.

Oliver wanted the red lollipop but just so he could punish everyone, for making him last to get one, he said stubbornly and ungratefully “green” then quickly snatched the green one. Nobody felt punished by this and instead they all found his choice amusing.

“What do you say boys?” ordered Mrs Robinson.

“Thank youuuu” answered the three brothers together as if they were reciting a boring times table.

Mirth flew among them as the doctor and Nurse Walton prepared to leave the house. He was very happy with events so far and although he wished he could fly to the next house and see the fun there, he still wanted to play with the three Robinson children and see what else developed.

Mirth knew some advanced spells for his age but hadn't yet learned to be in two places at the same time. He’d need to learn time travel magic for that, and youngling fairies were strictly forbidden from learning that kind of magic. Time travel spells could cause all kinds of trouble so only very senior fairies were allowed to learn them.

Besides, whatever the doctor was going to find on his next visit was for Glee to enjoy and Mirth was sure Glee would tell them all about it later.

Just at that moment, a senior fairy called Wiseacre hovered unseen near the youngling.

Wiseacre was just as invisible to Mirth as Mirth was to all the humans. He gave an invisible smile and a happy nod as he knew what Mirth was thinking and approved of his self-discipline in not trying to learn dangerous spells.

Mirth was heading for some trouble for using naughty magic today, but it was the kind of mischief that youngling fairies were expected to get up to in their free time. So although there would be consequences for the four friends, Wiseacre was there to oversee things and make sure they didn't get out of hand. And if he also enjoyed the spectacle of the mischief then that was just a happy coincidence.

Saying goodbye for the moment, Doctor Clayton and Nurse Walton left the Robinson house and headed to the home of the Sangfroids; who were the Robinson's next-door neighbours.

As Doctor Clayton and Nurse Walton left the Robinson's house and the door closed behind them, they smiled to each other when they heard Mrs Robinsons' quiet but annoyed voice.

"David Robinson, come here this instant . . ."

"He can be a one that David" said Doctor Clayton. "A nice lad but he certainly can be a one."

CHAPTER 15

# The Sangfroid Family

"Quite a first day you are having eh Jenny!" said the doctor encouragingly as they stepped out into the Robinsons' cool but sunny front garden.

"Whoever said the countryside was dull has never been to Cuckoo Village" she answered with a smile that told him not to worry about her.

"Indeed" nodded the doctor with a long raising of his eyebrows.

Doctor Clayton liked Nurse Walton, she always thought about others and tried to encourage them even if it was her that has having a difficult time.

What was also strange about this case was the fact that a boy waking up green, even his hair, eyes, teeth, fingernails, and pyjamas, should be alarming, but for some reason he felt quite calm. Doctor Clayton didn't quite think it in his head, but he felt in his heart that there was magic in the air. Of course, what he didn't know was that Mirth had whispered this to him while he was in the house giving Oliver a check-up.

The Sangfroid family lived next door to the Robinsons. Their house, at number six, Cuckoo Village, was set by its self but the front gardens of both houses didn't have a fence or a hedge to separate them.

There used to be a fence separating the two front gardens, but when their children were younger Mr & Mrs Robinson and Mr & Mrs Sangfroid had decided to remove it so the children could play together in a larger, shared front garden where their parents could keep an eye on them. Now that their children were old enough that they didn't need to be watched all the time, they had just left the garden that way.

The lush, green front lawn that stretched in front of both houses was well kept and tidy except for a small scooter that lay on its side under the Sangfroid's front window.

Doctor Clayton could have led Nurse Walton over the lawn, but he always felt that it was rude to walk so closely past people's front windows, so he took the time to walk up the Robinsons' garden path, through the gate then along the pavement to the Sangfroid's gate.

He wondered if the postman also did this and looked over the small front hedge to see if there was a trail of worn-out grass that would show if someone was walking the same path over it every day. He was coming to the conclusion that there was no trail so the postman must feel the same way he does, when Mr and Mrs Sangfroid opened their door and rushed up their garden path to open the little gate for them.

They rushed but at the same time tried to look as normal as possible, so they looked like they were in a walking race. The fact that they tried so hard to hide their rushing had the opposite effect and attracted even more attention to them than just openly running would have done.

Mr Evans, a few houses down, was toodling around at the front of his shop. It usually took him just a moment to close up in the mid-morning, but this particular morning he had been closing the shop for over twenty minutes. He was checking for loose pieces of stone in the wall and whatever else he could think of to keep him where he could watch the comings and goings of Doctor Clayton and Nurse Walton. When he saw the strange way the Sangfroids fast walked to their gate, both his eyebrows stood to attention and he nodded while softly humming as if his eyebrows had just reported some discovery to him.

"Something is definitely afoot" he said thoughtfully under his breath.

Mr Evans always fancied himself to be a detective when there was a mystery in the village. He liked to use phrases such as 'afoot' because he thought it sounded investigative. Something was indeed afoot, he just didn't know what . . . yet.

"Doctor, thank you so much for coming. Max, Max I, Oh doctor come quickly it's the strangest thing" fretted Mrs Sangfroid.

"Hello Mrs Sangfroid, this is Nurse Walton" replied the doctor as if everything were just fine.

The more worried patients were, especially parents of children, the more the doctor liked to put them at ease by acting as if there was nothing to be alarmed about at all. He found that mundane, everyday things were comforting to patients so instead of getting excited himself and worrying patients even more, he tended to break away from the subject for a while and keep up the usual polite conversation.

"Hello Mr and Mrs Sangfroi . . . . . " Nurse Walton tried to say, but before she could finish her greeting, she was cut off by a very loud screech which came from the still open front door of the Sangfroid house.

Everyone suddenly turned and stared as the screech, which was a child's voice, was repeated again and then again only much louder and longer. Even Mr Evans heard it from down the road aways and both he and his eyebrows stood to attention in the hopes that he could peer over the four adults in the front garden and see what was afoot in the house.

They all realised that it wasn't just a screech, it was a sentence, but it was screeched so high and so loud that it took a second and third screeching for them to catch what was being . . . screeched.

CHAPTER 16

# The Screecher

"I'mmm notttttt the devvvvvviiilllll!" came the extremely long, loud and angry screech again. Then there was a sound like thunder and "I'm notttttt the devvvvvvillllllllllll!" screeched yet again but this time sounding different; like the screecher was now running while screeching.

The Sangfroid's open front door led directly onto the staircase, and the cause of the thundering sound soon became clear as three children wildly scrambled down the stairs as they ran for dear life.

Despite the obvious assistance of gravity, they had trouble getting down the stairs as quickly as you might expect. They were all laughing so hard that they were finding it difficult to actually run and also keep to their eyes open and see where they were going.

As well as laughing their heads off, they also seemed to be in such knee-buckling fear of what was chasing them that they lost all strength and were blindly and chaotically scrambling to get ahead by dragging each other back in order to get a boost forward. This had the effect of wedging the three of them stuck between the wall on one side of the narrow staircase and the wooden banister rails on the other.

There was a secondary reason for the shirt-pulling-boost too. If one should happen to pull on the other back so hard that they got caught, then all the better as the screecher chasing them might be satisfied with just that one victim and stop chasing the puller/booster. It's always wonderful in life when you get a secondary benefit to something you do isn't it.

Suddenly free of the confines of the staircase, three of the four Sangfroid children exploded out of the house and into the garden.

The two eldest girls, Samantha and Sally Sangfroid, who were eleven and ten years old, immediately darted left. As their fear turned to joy, they celebrated by dancing a jig on the lawn.

Wesley Sangfroid, who was only seven years old, made a beeline straight for his mother and tried to use her legs as a shield from whatever horror was chasing him.

Samantha and Sally were laughing loudly as they continued to dance their jig, which, if a dance could be translated into words, it would be something like 'nye, nye, ne nye nye come and get me'.

Wesley's enjoyment of his fear of the beast was a little less sure than that of his big sisters. Oh, he enjoyed it alright but there was also a small child's still not being clear about what is and isn't truly dangerous. A mum or a dad to hide behind usually made up for the fact that he wasn't as brave (or foolish) as his two big sisters. Now that he was safely behind his mum he peeked back to see if the beast had emerged.

When the screeching terror did emerge, it shocked Doctor Clayton and Nurse Walton even more than their first sight of the real Oliver had.

What they saw was a screaming, volcanically angry little boy running at them waving an oversized yellow, plastic baseball bat above his head . . . . he was also totally, completely red.

What they didn't see or hear was Glee flying fast to keep up with the volcanically angry and totally red screecher all the while shouting "Chaaaarrrge" and "Get emmmmm" into his ear.

"I'm nottt the devvvillllllll!" the volcano continued to screech as he look around frantically for the nearest brother or sister within whopping distance. This was Wesley, who with no concern for his mum, was praying that her legs would withstand the torrent of bashes that were about to come.

Mr Sangfroid quickly stepped forward and expertly grabbed the yellow bat with his left hand and scooped up the eight-year-old screecher with his right arm in one flowing, well-practiced action.

The screecher's name was Max Sangfroid and although he was red and not green like Oliver Robinson, what was the same but different was the fact that his hair, eyes, teeth, tongue, fingernails and yes, even his pyjamas were red. His socks were blue, but he didn't sleep in his socks and had put them on after he got out of bed.

"Awww" moaned Glee as he flew to a stop above them all. He was disappointed that his charging volcano had been halted as he was sure that the further thrashing that Max would have given his brother and sisters would have made the best story of the day when he met up with his friends.

Glee noticed that little Max was so angry and had such single-minded determination to whop is sisters and brother with the plastic bat that he wasn't paying attention to his mouth and nose. As he wriggled and kicked in his father's arms, he dribbled and bubbled saliva from his mouth, and snot from is nose.

“Ewwwwe, Maaaaax” teased Samantha as she stopped her jig for a moment to draw attention to Max’s angry dribbling.

“Well, that’s not bad. Let’s see if Mirth can beat that” Glee said delightedly to himself as he looked at the angry dribbler and consoled himself about the failed whopping.

Mr Sangfroid dropped the plastic bat and held the kicking, screeching, wriggling Max with both arms. Max had been making a dash for his younger brother Wesley, but had now noticed his two elder sisters who were still dancing on the lawn and he was angrily kicking and wriggling in their direction.

"Daaaaaaddd they keep saying I'm the devilllllll. Get them." Max pleaded under the impression that it would be perfectly reasonable for his Dad to hear this then decide to join him in the attack.

"I know, I know Maxy. Don't listen to them" replied Mr Sangfroid as he gave Max a long, warm hug to calm him down.

Then to the dancing elder sisters who were making horn signs on their heads as they danced, "Silly Sally Sangfroid stop teasing your brother, you too Samantha".

"Yeah, silly Sally Sang - froid" shouted Max angrily. He said the name Sangfroid in an especially angry way, forgetting for the moment that it was his name too.

"What about Samantha?" protested Sally laughing and pretending to be angry because she had been called 'Silly Sally' and her elder sister had just been called 'Samantha' as if this meant that she was more to blame.

"Both of you, and you too Wesley, leave him alone" added Mrs Sangfroid as she shot Mr Sangroid a disapproving look for calling Sally 'Silly Sally'.

Max was calming down a bit, but not much.

"I'm NOT the devil am I dad?" he exclaimed.

"No Maxy, you're my screechy little angel" answered Mr Sangfroid as he tickled the pouting red boy.

Max laughed aggressively as if his dad's reassurance also meant that he was in the right about everything, which would include his desire to give his sisters and brother a further whopping with his bat.

It probably wouldn't have hurt them even if he could have caught them as it was an oversized bat made of very thin plastic and was almost like hitting someone with a balloon, almost. Still, Max had learned how to make it hurt. You had to really get a good swing and make sure the end and not the middle whopped them. He knew that because he'd practiced on them whenever he was angry at something; which was quite often. His practice told him that if he whopped them ten times, he would get nine laughs and one 'ow'.

He still hadn't given up on the idea though and kept an eye on the yellow bat that was now lying on the garden path. He relaxed to try to trick his dad into letting him go and planned a complicated 'break free, grab the bat and whop both of his sisters in one smooth motion' manoeuvre. His dad knew him too well and disguised his keeping him prisoner with a long hug.

This wasn't really so bad. He'd rather be whopping his sisters with the bat of course, but a hug is always nice. In an ideal world he would break free, whopp Wesley and his sisters with the bat then get a hug off his dad for doing a good job.

Unfortunately, this wasn't possible as Mr Sangfroid

kept the hug going as he talked to the doctor and nurse Walton. So, as he had no choice, Max begrudgingly settled for his dads loving hug; he could always whop his brother and sisters later. He probably would too because he had a long memory when it came to things he was angry about. Sometimes though, it wasn't that he had a long memory, it was just that, when he was angry, he stayed angry for a very long time, so the desire to whop someone never went away.

Glee hovered around Max and whispered into his ear. "Wait Maxy, relax, control yourself and calm down . . . but not too much. Don't forget the whopping. After all, they certainly deserve it."

As with Max, Glee hadn't given up on his plan to end his visit to the Sangfroid home with a bang, and a bash and of course lots of whops.

Max was impatient to punish Wesley and his sisters, but it occurred to him that if he managed to be patient and delayed the pleasure of the few whops he could probably manage to give them now, he could have a chance to give them a much more complete whopping later when dad wasn't around to save them. So, without knowing where it came from, he took Glee's advice and forced himself to calm down . . . a bit.

## CHAPTER 17

# Patient

Doctor Clayton and Nurse Walton had been shocked to see a shy little green boy in the Robinson's home when Oliver presented himself after playing a trick on them with the face painted Jonathan. But they were more shocked to see an angry little, red, scree . . . well, to see Max come screeching at them with the baseball bat held high in optimum whopping position. The bright yellow bat stood out as everything else connected to Max above his ankles was very, very red.

Somehow the little red screecher was more of a shock to see than the pouty, green Oliver had been. Red often meant danger (especially this time for Wesley, Sally and Samantha), but green could have a somewhat soothing effect on people; like a grassy meadow or the doctors beloved Morris Minor Traveller. In fact, the doctor had preferred red when he first bought the car but decided it wasn't the best colour for a car that is sometimes used to transport sick or even injured people so had settled for green.

When Max had calmed down a little, they took him into the house and the doctor looked him over in the same way as he had done with Oliver and with the same results.

"Hmmm" hummed the doctor, concentrating and talking to himself "nothing wrong here, as fit as young Oliver. Most intriguing"

"Is Oliver Robinson red too doctor?" asked a surprised Mrs Sangfroid with her mouth stuck open.

"Ah erm" Doctor Clayton stalled.

Doctors weren't supposed to tell anyone the details of other patients, so he considered giving Mrs Sangfroid the same evasive answer that he had to Mr Evans. Then he changed his mind and just came out with it.

"Green. Same in every way; only green," he answered.

Then, as Nurse Walton picked up on the doctor's openness, she added, "and well, y'know . . . not so angry."

"Oh, that part isn't new" grinned Mr Sangfroid sheepishly.

The doctor was beginning to sense that finding a medical answer might be a challenge. He knew a lot about how to fix people, but he'd lived long enough to know that sometimes knowledge alone wasn't always what was required to solve some problems.

'Some good old-fashioned wisdom was needed here he thought'. Being open about the problem and giving out information about the other patients in the village might prompt someone else to have an idea.

Brainstorming it was called. Sometimes it worked and sometimes it didn't. It certainly didn't hurt to try. Although, when he was a child and had tried this way to find an answer to something and it didn't work, his little sister had always called it 'a brainstorm in a teacup'. That had been her way of teasing him for not finding an answer.

"Green, hair and everything? Goodness me, whatever could be causing it, and why has only one child got it" Mrs Sangfroid wondered aloud.

Max just sat there sulking and looking from one adult to the other as he impatiently wondered when they were going to be done inspecting him so he could get back to the important business of whopping certain people.

"Don't worry, that's what we're here to find out" said Nurse Walton encouragingly.

"Yes, nodded the doctor. We have to stop by a couple of other houses then we'll pop back."

“Other houses? Goodness, how many other cases are there? And what colours?” mused Mr Sangfroid, not really expecting an answer from the doctor.

"Should we pack Maxy's overnight things, you know, in case we have to go to the H.O.S.P.I.T.A.L?" whispered Mrs Sangfroid dramatically.

Doing so had the same effect as Mr and Mrs Robinson fast-walking to their garden gate to meet the doctor and Nurse Walton and a now alert Max looked concerned even though he couldn’t work out the word from the spelling.

Samantha and Sally were still in the garden but were looking into the living room through the partially open window. Seeing that Max became suspicious when his mum was suddenly whispering and spelling a word, Samantha realised there was more fun to be had.

"Wow mum, that's very good. I didn't know you could spell HOSPITAL!" shouted Samantha, still skipping on the spot despite her legs beginning to ache.

Sally laughed at her sister’s jest but Wesley, now in the living room and still clinging to his mom, looked confused. Max was confused too but he also started to boil again as he sensed that he was being plotted against. Besides, he generally liked to be near boiling point just in case he needed to suddenly be angry at something.

“I don’t want to go to the hospital” moaned Max.

"Samanthaaaaaaa" growled Mrs Sangfroid through teeth that seemed to be glued together.

"I think we can hold off on that Mrs Sangfroid" answered the doctor as he patted Max on the arm. "We shan't be long. Let's see what's what with the other children first."

"Very well doctor, whatever you think best" she said, as always, accepting his advice.

This calmed Max down a little and Nurse Walton distracted him further by producing her white paper bag of lollipops and holding it out for Max to choose one. Max didn’t hesitate and he didn’t seem to care much what colour lollipop he grabbed either. He just snatched an orange one, peeled back the wrapper with a determined look on his face then stuffed it in his mouth.

Nurse Walton smiled at this, then turning and leaning around Mrs Sangfroid a little, she also held out the bag to Wesley.

“Why don’t you take one for each of your sisters too Wesley” she said kindly.

“They shouldn’t get any, they’re bad” complained Max in a garbled voice as he held his lollipop in place between his clenched teeth and his left cheek.

Wesley grabbed three lollipops but didn’t dare unwrap one in front of Max. Instead, he just held them while keeping an eye on his seemingly calm yet still very red brother.

Mr and Mrs Sangfroid then walked with Wesley and Max to the garden gate as Doctor Clayton and Nurse Walton left them and headed across the road to the

Vauxhall family's house. As they did this, encouraged by an invisible, excited and very naughty Glee, Max drew on all his practice at pretending not to be angry when he really still was. He put on his best 'I'm a happy little boy smile' and was convincing enough for his dad to loosen his grip and at this moment his head took on a naughty leer.

## CHAPTER 18

# A Well-Deserved Whopping

Suddenly, the Screecher came alive and before anyone knew what was happening, he had the yellow bat and was whopping his two older sisters again and again. Glee was clinging to the handle of the bat too as he imagined he was the one holding the bat and whacking the two sisters.

"Yahooooo Maxy, whop them good!" hollered Glee.

"I'm notttt the devillll, silly Sally Sangfroidddddd. I'm notttt the devillll silly Samantha Sangfroidddddd, you arrrrrre!" screeched Max again and again and again as he whopped once for each word he screeched.

Even though he was swinging wildly, he was making sure that the tip of the inflated plastic bat, which was the slightly harder bit, was doing the whopping. He was also doing a good job of changing the whopping angle so his two sisters couldn't defend themselves well.

Sally and Samantha were starting to hurt a bit but the sight of their red little brother thrashing away at them and the funny, balloony bopping sound the bat made when it hit them made them laugh - especially when it was the other being hit. They laughed so much that they had no strength to run away, fight back or even hold up their hands and defend themselves.

Whenever Sally or Samantha got an especially good balloony sounding whop to the head, the other laughed so hard that snot and tears erupted from their own nose and eyes. Then their laughing the sight of this made them even more helpless as Max took advantage and gave an especially angry whopping to whichever snotty, tear-streaked sister was more paralysed with laughter.

The fact that they seemed to be enjoying it made Max even angrier and redder. So, the whopping went on and on and got harder and harder until Max started to get tired.

Mr Sangfroid himself found the sight so funny that he forgot to step in and stop it. He was laughing hard until an annoyed Mrs Sangfroid marched past him to separate them.

"Snot from three. Woo hoo it's got to be a record" declared a proud, wide-eyed Glee.

It was the best fun Glee could remember having. That was saying a lot because he was very good at having fun. Glee wasn't cruel but he wasn't delicate either. Like most fairies his age, Glee loved to play rough sometimes. He and Mirth would often wrestle. It would usually start with one sneaking up on the other and giving him a good kick in the pants then running away terrified.

They loved each other and were the best of friends though, so they always controlled their emotions and were careful never to hurt each other when playing. Mirth was stronger than Glee but Glee was sneakier. So Mirth got the better of him in a straight wrestling match but Glee won when it was time for a sneak attack. He wished Mirth was here now as they could both be on the same side and help little Maxy whop his sisters.

Mr and Mrs Sangfroid could see that no real harm was being done, so Mrs Sangfroid halted. She thought Max getting tired from giving the whopping was the best way to calm him down, so she let take his revenge for a while longer.

Wesley was less relaxed. He wondered if they were going to let Max whop him too, so he decided that he had three options. The first was to continue hiding behind his mother but as neither his mum nor dad seemed interested in rescuing Samantha and Sally, he lost confidence in their protection.

His second option was, of course, to beg, but that never worked with Max when he was angry. He was a kind older brother to Wesley when he wasn't angry and always shared his sweets even though Wesley didn't always share when he was the only one to have any. When Max was angry though, which was quite often, it was a different story. Now he was as angry as Wesley had ever seen him, and that is saying something. He decided that begging Max not to whop him wouldn't work, so he took the third option and ran off to hide.

Wesley was good at hiding; he'd had lots of practice. He'd had about the same amount of practice at hiding as his dad had at grabbing Max and scooping him up. He had memorised all the best hiding places that were within dashing distance inside and outside the house. As they were already in the front garden, he headed for his favourite hiding place in the back garden.

Getting down on his hands and knees, Wesley climbed into the doghouse. Their dog, Ruby Sangfroid, wasn't jealous that Wesley was using his doghouse; he was excited as he had been tied up and had been pulling at the rope to see what all the noise was about but hadn't been able to get far enough to see around the corner.

Ruby jumped up and down while barking then ran into the doghouse and started to lick Wesley's face. Wesley protested this affection and was worried that Ruby would give his hiding place away if the Screecher came looking for him.

"Get away Ruby" Wesley hissed trying to sound angry and quiet at the same time. Ruby refused to leave though, and Wesley settled for just hiding behind him. 'At least it will be hard for Max to whop me in here if he does find me as he only ever whops us and never Ruby' he thought.

## CHAPTER 19

# The Vauxhall Family

After leaving the Sangfroid's garden, Doctor Clayton and Nurse Walton didn't comment on what they had just witnessed. Instead, Nurse Walton just looked at the doctor and raised her eyebrows in wonder and the doctor did the same in agreement.

Then as the doctor and Nurse Walton crossed Cuckoo Village's only road, Nurse Walton noticed the unusual order in which each house was numbered. The order was unusual in that there didn't seem to be any order at all. The houses weren't numbered like most streets with 1,3,5 etc on one side and 2,4,6 on the opposite side. Instead, at least on the east side of the village that they were in, the side of the road they had just left with the Robinson's and the Sangfroid's houses were numbered 11, 3, 6 then 12, and the houses on the side they were crossing to were numbered 1, 8, 5 then 4.

"What an unusual way of numbering the houses" she said.

"I hadn't really thought about that," said the doctor. Then, "well, some of the houses in the village are very old. So, as houses were built on both sides of the road in various places and at different times, they numbered them with whatever number came next I suppose - even though that isn't in order."

"So, the houses are numbered in order of when they were built over hundreds of years then?" asked Nurse Walton.

“Hmm, yes, I think so” answered the doctor.

“It must confuse the postman” she wondered aloud. “why don’t they re-number them so it goes house by house?”

“I suppose it’s because people become attached to their history and traditions and like familiar things, so even if some older things can be a bother sometimes, they are willing to live with the nuisance of it” he mused.

Nurse Walton nodded as this made sense to her. Then, with a cheeky smile, she said “like you and your car.”

Doctor Clayton pretended to be a bit sad at this but then smiled and said, “you know, I think you might have something there.”

Then they were at the garden gate of the Vauxhall family house. They could still hear the Screecher screeching and whopping away with the bat, as well as a dog excitedly barking even further in the distance. Nurse Walton smiled at the doctor then said, "let's see what's behind door number three."

Even though it was actually number four, Cuckoo Village, Doctor Clayton smiled back as he lightly knocked.

Before the doctor could knock his usual three times the door was quickly opened, so his third knock missed the door. Mrs Vauxhall opened the door wide and with a kind but concerned smile she hurriedly invited them both in.

"Good morning doctor. Thank you so much for coming, you too nurse . . ?" said Mrs Vauxhall.

As she greeted them, she shook Nurse Walton's hand but not Doctor Claytons who she'd known all her life having grown up nearby in Plumton before recently moving to Cuckoo Village.

"It's Jenny, Jenny Walton Mrs Vauxhall. It's very nice to meet you. It's Victoria isn't it, how is she?" Nurse Walton greeted back.

"She's in the living room, it's through here. She's . . . " said Mrs Vauxhall not knowing how to finish the sentence.

"Don't worry Mrs Vauxhall", the doctor assured her, "some of the other children, they're . . . .y'know, also."

"Oh really? Well then, anyway here she is" replied Mrs Vauxhall feeling a little relieved that it was a shared problem.

Then she turned and led them through the entrance hall and into the living room.

"Vicky, Doctor Clayton is here to see you" said Mrs Vauxhall making an extra effort to be cheerful for Vicky as she ushered them through.

CHAPTER 20

# Victoria Vauxhall

Victoria Vauxhall didn't look happy at all. Usually nine-year-olds are bouncing all over the house, but Vicky was sitting in the living room looking out of the window with the saddest expression on her face. She turned to look at them but didn't smile.

Vicky wore a beautiful purple ribbon in her hair, cute denim dungarees and oversized rabbit slippers . . . she was also totally, completely blue.

She had blue hair, blue eyes, blue teeth and even blue fingernails. She had blue slippers, but the slippers had always been that colour. She had told her mother 'I don't care about that stuff' when they were slipper shopping and her mother had suggested a 'cute' colour and held up some pink rabbit slippers.

Nurse Walton and Doctor Clayton had trouble getting used to the unusual sights that were greeting them in each home. There are all kinds of beautiful colours of people in the world. There were brown, black, white, caramel and in the case of Farmer Crabtree's cheeks, even pinkish people, but deepest green, bright red and now vibrant blue . . . including hair, eyeballs, teeth, and even fingernails was a sight that neither of them had seen before.

## CHAPTER 21

# Shimmer Meets Vicky

When Shimmer had first seen Vicky peacefully sleeping earlier that morning, she had given her a kiss on the forehead and watch as her spell took effect. What she didn't expect was that her child would look sad after she had woken up.

Shimmer had been a little disappointed at this and wondered if the spell had gone wrong. She decided it hadn't as, although it was a difficult spell to arrange, it was actually a simple one and fairies can always feel it when a spell doesn't quite work as it should.

'Ooo I bet the others have a more exciting human to play with' she thought. Then later when she heard a riot of screeching and laughing across the road, she had pressed her little fairy nose against Vicky's bedroom window to see what was going on.

Shimmer had watched as Glee burst into the Sangfroid's garden and steered the little red boy towards the other children he seemed to want to bash with a giant yellow balloon bat.

"That's not fair" she had said as she tapped a tiny fist against the glass. "They get all that fun and what am I supposed to do with little miss bluebell here" she had sulked.

Shimmer had sat with her chin resting on her hands and watched Vicky as she had woken up. She had hoped for some fun when Vicky went to brush her teeth and had first saw herself in the mirror.

That was disappointing too. Instead of a scream, Vicky had just stood there staring at her own blue face for what seemed the longest time. Then, in a not particularly excited or concerned manner, Vicky had said loudly enough so her mother downstairs could just about hear "Mum, I'm blue."

"Don't worry dear, I'll make your favourite for breakfast to cheer you up" Mrs Vauxhall had called back up thinking that Vicky was saying she was sad; as usual.

Then, without answering, Vicky had just gone ahead and brushed her blue teeth, washed her blue face, brushed her blue hair, and got dressed in her already blue dungarees and rabbit slippers.

Shimmer did get some fun out of seeing Mrs Vauxhall's reaction to actually seeing Vicky's unusual appearance. Vicky had passed her mother on her way down the stairs as her mother came up. Mrs Vauxhall had just stood frozen for a while before suddenly turning to run down the stairs to call the doctor.

Shimmer had laughed at this and flown down to listen in on the phone conversation. After that though not much had happened.

Poor Shimmer had spent the morning so far feeling cheated as she watched Vicky eat breakfast then just sit by the window occasionally writing in a little notebook she kept by her side.

On top of that, she had to see all the fun Glee was having. 'And I bet Mirth and Twinkle are having a great time too' she complained to herself.

Then, it was as if a wise invisible fairy had whispered in Shimmer's ear as she was inspired by a thought.

'Could it be that humans influence fairies as much as

fairies influence humans,' she thought.

Shimmer well knew that fairies could influence the thoughts and emotions of humans they had a particularly strong connection with, but it had never occurred to her that the other way around might also be possible.

"Oh, am I feeling sorry for myself because I'm being affected by little Miss Bluebell? Hmpph, we'll see about that" Shimmer said to herself in a determined voice.

From that moment, Shimmer set herself to winning the battle of influence and doubled her efforts to cheer both herself and Vicky up.

From then on, something strangely wonderful and perhaps even magical started to happen to Shimmer. She started to get a very warm feeling towards Vicky. At first, she had just been concerned about her own fun. Shimmer wasn't really a selfish fairy but like anyone young, fairy or human, she sometimes focused strongly on her own needs.

As Vicky had sat quietly eating breakfast and not complaining about the fact that she was totally, completely blue, Shimmer had started to notice what a beautiful little girl this Victoria Vauxhall was. Shimmer had sat and admired how kind and gentle her little blue face looked and how she always tried to comfort her mother as Mrs Vauxhall paced around waiting for the doctor to arrive.

'What a good little girl Vicky is' Shimmer had thought. 'If only Twinkle could be as good as her' she then smiled to herself; not for a moment considering that she herself was only slightly less naughty than Twinkle.

In time, Shimmer developed very warm feelings towards Vicky. Before she knew it, she was far more concerned about the little girls' happiness than she was about having fun herself.

Shimmer knew that fairies can affect what humans think and even feel, and that was part of what they were practicing today; as well as having mischievous fun of course. But what Shimmer was also learning today was that humans can certainly affect fairies.

Mrs Vauxhall's love and care for little Vicky radiated throughout their home and Shimmer could feel it everywhere. Not only in Vicky's heart, but in the walls and tables, chairs and everything in the home. It was like a golden glow that could be felt but not seen.

As Shimmer had the same kind of caring heart, she had picked up on this and soon began to feel the same way towards this blue little girl. Before long, Shimmer was doing everything she could to cheer Vicky up and make her smile and as Shimmer had the most beautiful singing voice of all fairies, she flew close to Vicky's ears and sang songs to her.

Shimmer wasn't good at making up songs or poems like Glee, but she was a better singer than him. She often made up nonsense songs but her friends never seemed to mind because her singing voice was so lovely and her tone was very kind and gentle (when she sang that is). Her friends sometimes joked and complained that she sounded so kind when she sang and asked why she couldn't sound like that when she talked also.

Shimmer sang a nonsense song to Vicky and although Vicky couldn't actually hear it, she somehow felt warm and happy for a while and even smiled for a moment.

*Blue Bell, Blue Bell.*

*Bell, Blue Bell.*

*Bell, Bell, Blue Bell.*

*Blue, Blue, Bell.*

*Vicky, Vicky don't be sad.*

*Vicky Blue Bell, Blue, Blue Bell*

## CHAPTER 22

# Green, Red and now. . .

Now that the doctor and Nurse Walton had arrived, Shimmer was happy as they both looked kind and that meant more people to help cheer up poor little Vicky.

Sitting beside Vicky, Nurse Walton bent her head to look into Vicky's eyes and with a kind smile said, "Hello Victoria, I'm Jenny, how are you feeling?"

Vicky felt shy and didn't answer except to continue staring down at her rabbit slippers and to give a slow shrug of her shoulders.

"Would you like a lolly pop?" asked Nurse Walton.

She then took out the white paper bag that was in her pocket and held it out to Vicky.

"These are my favourites. Some people like to give one to good little girls after a check-up but I sometimes like to give one before. I think there might even be a blue one in there" she said encouragingly.

Vicky hesitated then after a quick look to her mother who smiled her approval, she reached in and took a red lolly pop but didn’t peel off the wrapper. Instead, she just held it in her lap.

"Oh dear, you must be feeling down if you don't scoff a lolly pop right away. I know some children in this village who would have bitten my hand of," joked Nurse Walton.

"Oliver Robinson I bet," said Vicky without smiling.

"And then Max Sangfroid would have bitten his hand off" she added with a glum smile and nod of her head.

"Well, if you don't want to have it now that's alright. You can save it for later. Here's something else to put in your mouth instead, I'm afraid it doesn't taste as nice as a lolly" said Nurse Walton.

Nurse Walton waved a thermometer in front of Vicky so she could see what she was talking about, but Vicky didn't turn to look at it or even move her head except to just open her mouth.

When Nurse Walton lodged the thermometer under Vicky's tongue, Vicky slowly closed her mouth and patiently endured the wait. Then Shimmer flew close to Vicky's face then settled on the very tip of the thermometer. From there she cupped her tiny hands to her mouth and shouted "Vickyyyyy look at meeeeee."

Of course, Vicky couldn't hear or see Shimmer, but somehow her mood suddenly felt a little better again and she made Nurse Walton smile by going cross-eyed as she tried to stare at the numbers that ran along the thermometer to where Shimmer was sitting.

When Shimmer saw that Vicky had responded to her call, she sat up straight with surprise and bit her lower lip in excitement.

“Ooooo, oooooo that’s a first time, woo hooooooo” howled an ecstatic Shimmer.

Shimmer was happy Vicky had done what she had suggested because it was her first success at directly influencing a human. Despite being a fairy and knowing some magic, influencing a human by whispering in their ear (or shouting as was more Shimmer’s style) was a great accomplishment for a fairy.

The true reason this was so special was because humans don't hear fairy words with their ears or mind, they hear them with their heart. And a human can only hear a fairy if the fairy and the human have what Mirth calls 'emotional resonance'. That means, if the human has a pure heart as the fairy does too. If they are both kind (even if they don't always show it) then their hearts match and it makes communication between a fairy and a human possible.

Vicky felt happy about this too, but she didn't know the real reason because she didn't have Mirth to teach her. So, when Vicky saw Nurse Walton smile, her heart warmed a little and she smiled too.

"That's better," said Nurse Walton.

"Yes it is" said Shimmer to herself.

"Is Mr Vauxhall away again?" asked Doctor Clayton.

"Yes he's been away for two months now. If his stays get any longer, we might as well all move with him" answered Mrs Vauxhall.

"Urrsttrs awaarrr wngr van herrrr" added Vicky.

"What's that deary?" asked Nurse Walton as she gently removed the thermometer and looked at the reading with a satisfied nod that told the doctor that Vicky's temperature was fine.

"I said, he stays there longer than he stays here" repeated Vicky clearly now that she had nothing in her mouth.

"Vicky knows that Daddy's job is important, but she misses him so much, and now this!" said Mrs Vauxhall feeling sorry for poor Vicky.

"I know, it can't be easy, but there are lots of children in the village for you to play with aren't there Vicky? Did you make friends with any of them yet?" asked Doctor Clayton.

"Sometimes" answered Vicky.

"When she's feeling down, she mopes around the house a lot. Likes to bury her nose in a book. The sadder she feels the less she feels like playing out with the other children. Also, the sadder she looks the less the other children want to play, and it's not so easy as she doesn't know them well yet" explained Mrs Vauxhall.

"A sombre circle" said Nurse Walton thoughtfully, meaning that feeling down can sometimes make the environment around you sad then that sad environment in turn makes you even more sad. Of course, it also works the opposite way when you feel happy.

Doctor Clayton waited while Nurse Walton finished her inspection of Vicky then told Mrs Vauxhall what he had told the other parents; that apart from being totally, completely blue, Vicky was as fit and healthy as any child her age should be.

There was only one other family in the village that had children and they were also on his list of visits.

"Let me finish my rounds Mrs Vauxhall then maybe we can see what's what. I'll pop back soon, and we can decide what's to be done. For now though, please don't worry too much, Vicky seems to be fine . . . of course, apart from being as blue as a blueberry."

"Or a bluebell" smiled Vicky.

At this, Shimmer sat to attention and bit her lower lip again in a wide grin.

“Yessss, oh I'm so good at this” she celebrated raising her two tiny fists above her head.

Mrs Vauxhall seemed to relax a little at the doctors'

reassurance and also on seeing Vicky's smile.

With that, Doctor Clayton and Nurse Walton left the Vauxhall home and again crossed the road. They turned left when they were at the other side and walked past the Quarner Shop and the little church and on to the old Vicarage which was the last house at the western side of Cuckoo Village.

## CHAPTER 23

# Flutterby

After the doctor and Nurse Walton passed the church, they came upon the front garden of a house that wasn't like the others. Some houses in the village didn't have a front garden. No one knows if the house or the road came first. So, there was only the pavement between the road and the front door of those houses. Then some houses were set back from the road, had little front gardens and a fence, a hedge or a wall around them.

The front garden of this house didn't have anything around it. It was an open and welcoming space. The garden wasn't big, but it was very beautiful. It had a small green lawn on either side of the path that curved its way to the front door. Two delightful flower beds ran along the outsides of the lawn and under the two front windows on either side of the door. Even the upstairs as well as the downstairs windowsills were decorated with flowering plants. It was immediately clear that whoever looked after this garden loved colourful plants and flowers.

As they approached the house, Twinkle flew out of an open window to greet them and as she did, she spotted a yellow and black swallowtail butterfly settled on a windowsill flower

Twinkle cooed at the beauty of the swallowtail and invited it to fly with her by singing a song that Glee had taught her.

*Butterfly, butterfly, dance with me.*
*Butterfly, flutter-by come and see.*
*Let us fly so high above*
*to seek a flower and drink its love.*
*If you come and join my flight,*
*your heart will fill with golden light.*

The butterfly could not hear the song, but it could feel it. Then forgetting the sweet nectar of the flower, it lifted off and fluttered along with Twinkle as she flew over to greet Doctor Clayton and Nurse Walton.

When Twinkle and the butterfly had danced around them for a moment, she sat lightly on the butterfly and rode it back towards the house as she sang her song again.

For the doctor and Nurse Walton, it was almost as if the butterfly was leading them to the front door. If it had been a bee, they might have swatted at it and ducked down while running away but butterflies where different. When a beautiful butterfly comes near people they usually try to keep as still or steady as possible in the hope that it will land on them. Butterflies and cats are similar in that way. You want a bee or a wasp to go away and you can call a dog to come to you, but a butterfly or a cat will only come when they want to, and people feel honoured and happy if they are chosen.

Of course, a cat can 'choose' to sit on your lap or on whatever book or newspaper you are reading at the table if it feels that you'd be far better off paying attention to 'it' while it ignored you as it slept. But if a cat tries to sit on your head as a butterfly sometimes does then you wouldn't feel so honoured.

Nurse Walton drew in her breath at the sight of the butterfly as well as the lovely garden. Somehow the butterfly dancing in the air in front of them seemed to bring the brightly coloured garden and lovely vicarage house even more to life than the colour and flowerbed patterns already did.

When Nurse Walton was younger, she always thought that flowers should sing or play music. She had sometimes put her ear close to their petals to see if she could hear anything. Of course, she always first checked to see if there was a busy bee within taking care of the flower before she leaned in to listen to it. She wouldn't want any poor bee to think a giant monster with an ear shaped mouth was closing in to gobble it up.

She never heard music coming from a flower but whenever she saw a butterfly hopping from flower to flower, she imagined that it could hear the music that flowers were making and that it wasn't just collecting nectar but was also dancing. So, when she saw the big yellow butterfly dancing ahead of them, she imagined the whole garden and the flowers on the front of the house were playing music that only the butterfly could hear.

Nurse Walton was almost right, as it was Twinkle's lovely singing voice that the butterfly was dancing to; even if the butterfly itself didn't know it.

"Oh! How lovely!" exclaimed Nurse Walton.

"You should see the back garden," said Doctor Clayton with pride, thinking it was the garden and not the butterfly she was complimenting.

As she was about to also compliment the garden, Nurse Walton let the doctor's response do for both.

“That too” she answered with a smile.

Even though it wasn't his garden, Doctor Clayton felt that the people of Cuckoo Village were his people, and he was always happy when someone else got to see what a lovely place the village was.

"Mr Saffron has green fingers" he added, meaning that he was a wizard when it came to growing things.

"So does Oliver," joked Nurse Walton with a naughty smile.

Doctor Clayton looked at her with an appreciative grin and a laughing Twinkle in and also near his eye.

Twinkle liked Nurse Walton’s joke and made a note to remember it so she could tell it to her friends later.

“Oh these are nice people aren't they swallowtail?” she said to the butterfly.

Of course, the butterfly couldn’t actually hear Twinkle, but she had decided to give it a name already as fairy folk like to play with creatures as much as with humans even if the creatures didn’t always know they had just acquired a new friend.

By the time the two visiting humans had followed Twinkle and the butterfly through the garden gate and were halfway down the path, they could see that the front door was already wide open. Curiously though, there were no panicking parents to greet them.

Nurse Walton wasn’t sure why, but she always felt that an open front door indicated a happy home. There was something pleasing to her about fresh, fragrant air from a flower garden breezing through the house and perhaps the occasional curious butterfly stopping by for a visit.

Through the open front doorway of the Saffron family home could be seen a wide hallway with a floral-patterned tile floor. In some wall-hanging pots there were many different kinds of flowering hanging-plants that poured down to the ground like waterfalls made from one half of a rainbow.

As Doctor Clayton and Nurse Walton reached the open front door, and Twinkle danced the butterfly on into the house and settled it atop one of the flowers of a Saffron plant, it almost felt like the garden continued on into the house.

Twinkle notice that the petals the butterfly landed on were a bit wilted and wondered why the butterfly hadn't chosen a brighter one to land on. Then as the butterfly finally rested, it seemed to wrap its large yellow wings around the blue flower as if it was giving it a hug to encourage it.

Before either Doctor Clayton or Nurse Walton could pull the string to ring the old-fashioned bell that hung on the doorframe, Mr Saffron appeared in the hallway holding a small watering can. He was just about to give Twinkle a shower when he spotted them and smiled in surprise to see them standing in the doorway.

"Oh, hello Doctor, Mrs Saffron told me you were in the village. We didn't expect you so soon" he said warmly welcoming them.

CHAPTER 24

# The Saffron Family

"Come in, come in" Mr Saffron encouraged like he didn't have a care in the world.

Nurse Walton gave the doctor a quick look to see if he might have the wrong house. The doctor's silent reply confirmed that they were indeed here to see the Saffron family and here is Mr Saffron standing in his own front hall. Only, in a far more relaxed state than the other parents.

"Thank you Mr Saffron" replied the doctor.

Doctor Clayton's tone was especially friendly because he liked Mr Saffron very much. Mr Saffron also liked Doctor Clayton too; especially because the doctor appreciated his garden so much.

"This . . . is Nurse Walton" the doctor continued.

Even though it was the fifth time that he had introduced Nurse Walton to a Cuckoo Villager that day, he still said it with warmth as he liked her very much and he also liked introducing people to his friends in Cuckoo Village.

"Hello Nurse, it's very nice to meet you" said Mr Saffron taking off a gardening glove and shaking her hand.

Mr Saffron's hand was a little rough but warm and soft, and his handshake was jolly and enthusiastic.

"It's nice to meet you too Mr Saffron" replied Nurse Walton as she shook his hand as vigorously as he was shaking hers. "Gosh, it's like heaven here, such beautiful plants," she added.

It was autumn, which was Mr Saffron's favourite time of year as far as gardening goes because that's when saffron plants flowered. He had become interested in gardening when he was a child after he had discovered that his family name, 'Saffron', was the name of a beautiful, late season flowering plant. The saffron plant usually had royal bluish/purplish petals with bright yellow/golden seeds within; what Mr Saffron referred to as 'their treasure'. So, although he loved the changing colour of golden autumn leaves as they began to fall and coat the ground, he liked that saffron flowers cheered everything up with such vivid colours just before everything settled down for a cold winter.

When he was a young boy, nursing plants and flowers had been considered an unusual hobby for a lad his age, and because his family name was 'Saffron' the other children at Mr Saffron's school in Plumton had given him the nickname 'Flower'.

You never know what logic or reasoning children will use when they give their friends a nickname. Flower was a strange nickname for sure and at first Mr Saffron didn't like it at all, but over time he got used to it and even came to like it. Mrs Saffron, who had gone to the same school as Mr Saffron, only one year below, sometimes still affectionately called him Flower. She was certainly happy that he loved gardening so much as her she always found herself surrounded by the most beautiful colours and fragrances both inside the house as well as outside.

Mr Saffron raised his head ever so slightly in

appreciation for Nurse Walton's compliment. He happily narrowed his eyes and pushed out his bottom lip a little in the kind of smile where the corners of the mouth go down instead of up.

It wasn't such a different expression than the suspicious one Mr Evans had given her as he and his eyebrow had checked to see if she was going to have a problem with the name of his Quarner Shop. However, some tiny difference in the way Mr Saffron down-smiled completely changed it into the warmest, welcoming smile she had ever seen.

"Hmmm, this one will do juuust fine" he said to Doctor Clayton while slowly nodding his head.

Doctor Clayton was very pleased with Nurse Walton so far today. She was kind, good with both parents and children and everyone seemed to like her very much. He was also happy with Mr Saffron's approval of her because he was pretty sure that, just like him, she would be going home with an armful of flowers and plants. He wouldn't tell her though. Mr Saffron would surprise her at the last moment as he always did with his guests.

"Well, come through, come through. Meet the Buddha" said Mr Saffron mysteriously. He spared Twinkle from a shower and put down the watering-can then marched further into the house.

They followed Mr Saffron into the hall and stopped at the second door on the left which was the entrance to the living room.

Further back in the hallway, Twinkle stuck out her hand out towards the butterfly and mimicked the humans.

"Nice to meet you too Mr Swallowtail. Now you stay here. I want to see their faces when they see my handiwork."

Then she flew across the hall, ahead of the doctor and Nurse Walton and on into the living room. Then she hovered there to enjoy their wonder at what they were about to encounter.

As soon as Mr Saffron had opened the door, it was already time for Doctor Clayton and Nurse Walton to be shocked . . . again.

## CHAPTER 25

# Heart of Gold

Little Chloe Saffron was sitting sideways on a chair by a window with both hands resting calmly on her lap and the autumn sun shining through the party open window onto her face.

The window overlooked their back garden which was larger and even more colourful than the front garden. Chloe's mother, Mrs Saffron, was brushing Chloe's waist length, silky hair with long, slow strokes of the brush.

Chloe, who was the same age as Vicky at nine years old, looked very peaceful and happy. On her feet she wore house slippers that looked a little like silver ballet dancers' shoes. She wore white stockings, a knee length purple skirt that was covered with pictures of sun flowers, and a yellow blouse which had a frilly collar. She was also totally, completely golden.

She had golden hair, golden eyes, golden teeth and tongue and even golden fingernails.

As she turned to face the four of them, her bright, golden face showered them with golden light.

The golden light that radiated from Chloe's face was very bright but for some reason it didn't dazzle them or make it difficult to see as it does when looking directly at the sun. They also didn't feel any heat from the light as you might feel in bright sunlight - but for some reason, they felt warmed inside by its glow.

“Oh my” declared an amazed Nurse Walton.

CHAPTER 26

# Making Stories

Earlier that morning, when Twinkle had first visited Chloe and cast her spell, she had the same reaction.

Chloe had still been sound asleep when Twinkle arrived, but it was getting close to the start of the day. So as Mirth had instructed, Twinkle flew very close to Chloe and gently kissed the forehead of the peacefully sleeping child.

"Rise and SHINE" said Twinkle with a giggle.

At that moment, all the magical power and stored up yellow golden colour Twinkle had absorbed from the rainbow transferred to Chloe and she took on a beautifully golden hue which also lit up the entire room. Then when the spell was complete, Chloe opened her golden eyes and gazed with wonder at the room around her without yet knowing that its transformation was the result of the golden light that she herself was emitting.

"Goodness me!" a delighted Twinkle had said to herself as she flew back and upward from for a better look at the sleepy, golden girl rising to get out of bed.

Then suddenly, the look of joy on Twinkle's face turned to one of annoyance as she scrunched up her nose. She saw two other fairies flit in through the bedroom window that Chloe's mother always opened slightly to help her daughter wake up.

Twinkle instantly recognised one of them as a sometimes co-troublemaker and sometimes rival and equally mischievous fairy called Scintilla. She guessed the other was her little brother who was called Finagle but everyone just called him Fin. Twinkle knew that Fin was always being dragged around by his big sister as she got up to mischief, so didn't blame him and instead focused intensely on Scintilla.

"Oi, Tilla, get out of it" demanded Twinkle.

At Twinkles sudden shout, Scintilla turned in alarm from her delight at discovering Chloe. Then she prepared herself for a challenge as she was a bold fairy and usually tried to bluff her way out of any trouble she found herself in. This was an instinctive reaction as she'd had a lot of practice.

"I found her, she's mine" insisted Scintilla.

She then put herself between Chloe and Twinkle and hovered defiantly with her fists on her hips.

"You found her?" snorted Twinkle. Then, "I MADE her!"

"You mean Mirth made her" replied Scintilla dismissively.

"I mean 'I' made her" asserted Twinkle as she mirrored Scintilla by putting her own fists on her hips.

"Now clear off and make your own story. And take Finkle with you!" she ordered with a stamp of her right foot even though there was nothing to stamp on.

"Finagle" corrected Fin sheepishly as he was a bit scared of Twinkle.

Twinkle felt a bit bad about bullying Fin as she knew it wasn't his fault, but she was angry at them for trying to steal her story and wanted to show them who was boss.

For a moment, Scintilla just glared at Twinkle as she considered standing her ground, or, air. It was no use though, she knew that although Twinkle was known for being a very sweet fairy, when she was cross, she could be quite fearsome. And the last thing any fairy wants is a cross Twinkle.

So, giving a loud and very dissatisfied "Hmphhh!" Scintilla turned to her worried looking brother and said, "come on Fin, we can find a better story at the watermill."

Fin's face lit up at this as he loved playing at the nearby watermill. Being quite young still, he was obsessed with fireflies and was always trying to play with them and make friends. There was always lots of fireflies near the watermill, so he took any chance to go there even by himself even though he still wasn't aloud to play out alone.

And with that, Scintilla flitted angrily out of the open window with Fin following. As she did so, she turned and shook her fist.

"I'll get you for this . . . Sprinkle" she shouted.

Twinkle laughed at this to show she wasn't worried.

"Any time, Splintilla!"

With that future encounter promised, little troublemaking Scintilla and her poor younger brother Finagle were gone.

As Scintilla flew off and Twinkle remained, they both laughed to themselves as they were mostly friends and their rivalry was all part of the fun of the friendship.

Shaking her head at the open window for a moment, Twinkle had then turned to again look at her wonderful prize.

"Ohhh, I bet I've got the best one!" she exclaimed to herself.

## CHAPTER 27

# The Final Inspection

In the downstairs hall facing the open doorway to the Saffron family living room, both Doctor Clayton and Nurse Walton stood mesmerised for a moment.

A deeply warm, golden glow poured from the room and even illuminated the ceiling and floor in the hallway. At first Nurse Walton wondered if there was a big fire heating their living room, but it wasn't really a cold day even though it had been raining during the night. Then she wondered if the golden glow pouring out of the living room might be because the Saffron family had decided to compete with Mr Evans and open a secret sweet shop.

In any case they were soon to get their answer as Mr Saffron ushered them in.

Unaware that a great battle between two fearsome fairies had occurred in his own house earlier that morning, Chloe's father stood alongside the doctor and Nurse Walton as the stepped into the living room.

"Good morning Chloe" said the doctor trying not to sound astounded.

"Hello" answered Chloe with a simple smile as if she didn't have a care in the world.

"I suppose you woke up to a bit of a surprise this morning eh Chloe?"

"Surprise?" said Chloe, for a moment really not sure what surprise the doctor could be talking about.

After thinking for a moment, she got his meaning.

“Oh, yes” she said with a smile.

Mrs Saffron stopped brushing Chloe's hair and answered instead.

"Er . . actually doctor, strange as it may seem, at first, we ahm, didn't quite notice that she was so . . . radiant."

Then she continued in an embarrassed and apologetic voice "I popped into Chloe's room at about seven thirty and for some reason just didn’t notice the glow. Chloe herself got up, washed then brushed her teeth, got dressed and came down for breakfast without noticing either. It wasn't until she had finished her breakfast that Mr Saffron mentioned that she looked a little brighter and, well, even happier than usual. Once he said that then it seemed obvious. Can't see how it took so long for us to notice that she was actually gold and radiating golden light. I don't know what's stranger, that Chloe's as golden as my wedding ring from head to toe or that it took us thirty minutes to notice it."

Mrs Saffron finished her tale, paused for a moment, then with a brief shrug of her shoulders went back to brushing Chloe's hair.

"Strange within strange" said Nurse Walton with an amazed look on her face.

"In-deed" agreed Doctor Clayton. Then "Oh, please excuse me Mrs Saffron, Chloe, this is Nurse Walton."

Nurse Walton, Chloe and Mrs Saffron greeted each other, then Nurse Walton looked over Chloe the same as they had the other three children and came to the same conclusion.

"Fit as a fiddle and cute as a button!" she declared with a smile and a nod.

Chloe giggled and Mrs Saffron smiled proudly at this.

Then Nurse Walton sat at the table besides Chloe.

"You have a big sister don't you Chloe? Angelica isn't it? Isn't she here?"

"She's at university. She only usually comes home at holidays," answered Chloe with a warmth that filled her eyes when she talked about her big sister.

"Angelica just started this year" added Mr Saffron.

"It's nice that you have a sister. I only had brothers and they always ganged up on me" said Nurse Walton.

"Hmmm," Chloe agreed about her sister "she always plays with me."

"With Angelica being so much older, it's almost as if Chloe had two mothers" added Mrs Saffron as she continued to brush Chloe's hair even though the job seemed to have been finished for a while already.

As she had finished her inspection, Nurse Walton took Chloe's left golden hand and gave it a gentle squeeze.

When she let go, Chloe opened her palm to find a blue lollipop there and she smiled as if Nurse Walton had done a magic trick.

Despite all the magic Twinkle was involved with that day, she was impressed too and gave a delighted "Ohhh".

Nurse Walton thought Chloe was the happiest and most beautiful child she had ever seen. She could feel something inside her own heart that wanted to love her and take care of her; almost as if Chloe were her own child.

Mr Saffron sat down and looked deep in thought, then asked.

"Well, doctor, little Buddha here isn't the only one

that you've looked over today eh. I assume there are other's blooming? So what do you make of it all?"

"It's a tough one alright. Green, red, blue and now gold. Four families, four children, four colours and not one of them has so much as a runny nose. I can't say for sure that medicine is going to be the answer to this one."

"Sometimes knowledge just isn't enough doctor. What we need is good old-fashioned wisdom if you don't mind me saying so" answered Mr Saffron.

Nurse Walton looked confused, but Mrs Saffron knew exactly what Mr Saffron was talking about and so did the doctor.

"I'll get Chloe ready Flower. You pick out a nice potted plant" she said as she finally stopped brushing Chloe's hair.

Then taking her totally, completely golden daughter by the hand, she stood up and said "come on Chloe love, we're going on a visit."

Doctor Clayton turned to Nurse Walton and said "Jenny, could you go get Vicky Vauxhall and I'll bring Oliver and Max. Let's all meet in front of the church in ten minutes. We have one more house call."

With that, Doctor Clayton and Nurse Walton left the Saffron house. Nurse Walton crossed the road and headed for the Vauxhall home, Doctor Clayton walked along the path, past the old church and the Quarner Shop and towards the Sangfroid and Robinson homes. Mrs Saffron fussed around Chloe as they got ready to leave the house and Mr Sangfroid hummed to himself as he went into the greenhouse in the back garden to select one of his very best plants as a visiting gift.

## CHAPTER 28

# Gathering Together

As the Saffron family lived closest to the meeting point at the church, Chloe and her parents arrived first, then Nurse Walton with Vicky and Mrs Vauxhall.

Vicky and Chloe stared at each other like they were looking into a mirror for the first time today. They knew each other a little from school but weren't friends yet even though they were the same age and lived in the same small village. Vicky and her family had only moved to Cuckoo Village one month earlier and Vicky had spent most of that time staying inside reading or just staring out of the window like a house cat.

"Hello Victoria" said Mrs Saffron as if there was nothing unusual about the little blue girl before her.

Then she added "why don't you say hello to Victoria, Chloe?" and gently pushed on Chloe's shoulder.

"Oh, ahm, hello Vicky" obliged Chloe.

"Hello" answered Vicky still staring at the golden Chloe as hard as Chloe was staring at her. Then suddenly, both of them started laughing; not quite at each other but at the general situation of them being the way they were.

Then, for something to talk about, other than their unusual appearance, Vicky sheepishly asked Chloe "Where are we going?"

Chloe stuck out the index finger of her left hand but kept the hand down by her side as she wagged the finger in the direction of the dirt path a few times and said in a low tone "I think we're going to the old ladies house".

Vicky didn't know who that was but was amused by the idea. She leaned to her right to look past Chloe but couldn't see a house because the tree lined path curved as it went along. She didn't ask who the old lady was as she liked mysteries and thought the path with the trees and bushes on either side looked very mysterious, so she enjoyed the intrigue of the impending visit.

Soon Doctor Clayton appeared, followed by Oliver Robinson, Max Sangfroid and both of their entire families except for Ruby Sangfroid.

Max had finished whopping Samantha and Sally with the plastic bat and had reluctantly agreed to leave it at home. He still kept an angry eye on them though and was trying to decide if he'd finished punishing them for the day.

Wesley had escaped the whopping from his brother but wasn't going to relax until a whole day had passed. He knew that Max was good at pretending to calm down so half expected his brother to 'get him' at any moment.

For a while everyone stared hard at the green, red, blue and gold children and even those children stared hard at each other. The family members who had gotten used to one of their own waking up an unusual colour now had a fresh surprise as they saw the others. Also, the sight of four of them together made it seem even stranger.

"Look, Max woke up red. Hey, you look great Max" said David Robinson who was genuinely impressed with how Max's appearance.

Max thought about David's compliment for a while and decided that there was no hint of a suggestion that he was the devil. He gave his big sisters a sideways 'take that' look, almost as if the compliment was a justification for the whopping he had given them.

Samantha didn't like this, so she answered, "look, David woke up ugly. Oh wait, he's always been ugly."

Some of the children and even a few of the adults laughed at this but David wasn't upset. Everyone knew he was a handsome boy, and he was used to Samantha and Sally's teasing him just as they were used to his teasing them.

Now that the Sangfroids and Robinsons had also arrived at the meeting point, they were all getting ready to follow Doctor Clayton to the old lady's house when Mr Evans 'happened' to be walking past the church.

He had been taking a very long time to close up his shop so as to have an excuse to stay outside longer and see what all the fuss was about. When his eyebrow had been alerted to the crowd gathering near the church, it had pulled him in their direction so it could check on things. Mr Evans' eyebrow was very suspicious of unusual goings on and wouldn't let poor Mr Evans rest until it had completed a thorough investigation.

When he drew closer to the group, he was trying hard to think of an excuse for suddenly joining them but as he had fast walked over out of concern he would miss something and have nothing to report to Mrs Evans, he hadn't thought of anything by the time he arrived.

Mr Evans always liked to pretend that he wasn't interested in what the people of his village got up to. 'People round ere like to keep to themselves and that's the way I likes it' he would say.

In reality, like an inquisitive grandfather, he loved the

people of Cuckoo Village and was always interested in who was doing what.

The entire group turned and looked at him as he approached, and this sudden group attention flustered him.

"Well, . . . I'm coming too" was all he could manage.

At this everyone smiled as they found his embarrassment to be charming; and anyway, everyone in the village liked him so they were happy to have him among their number.

“You’re quite welcome Mr Evans” said Mr Saffron in a kindly voice.

Still embarrassed but feeling welcomed by the group, Mr Evans and his eyebrow settled down again as the smiles around him calmed them both down.

Now that his eyebrow was relaxed and satisfied that nothing suspicious was going on, it was both of his eyeballs turn to stand to attention as he suddenly jutted his head forwards a little when he noticed some of the brightly coloured children. His eye widened and he just stared at them as most people did when they first saw them.

Being a patient man when needed, Mr Evans turned to Mr Robinson.

"well, let's see what this is all about then shall we."

Mr Robinson smiled and replied “that's just what we’re about to do”.

"Lead the way Mr Saffron" called out Doctor Clayton.

"Right-ho doctor," answered Mr Saffron enthusiastically. Then he turned away from the group and towards the path they were about to take.

"Okay Cuckoo'ers, here we go."

# CHAPTER 29

# A Short Walk

Mr Saffron had selected a kentia palm as his visiting gift for the old lady. Her house was down the path and among the trees in a spacious grove that stretched from the back of the church to the stream at the bottom of Farmer Crabtree's cow field.

The kentia was a beauty; almost as tall as Mr Saffron himself. He carried the pot against his belly and the palm leaves swayed around above his head. As the four families, Doctor Clayton, Nurse Walton and Mr Evans walked behind him they looked like an army on parade following a leafy flag bearer.

The road and pavement that ran through Cuckoo Village was stone and as old as the village itself, but the side road that led to the old lady's house was just a grassy path. It looked like it didn't get used much and there were worn-out area that the wheels of her car left when she took the occasional drive to Plumton.

"Why are we going to the old lady's house?" asked a nervous Wesley Sangfroid to no one in particular.

"I bet it's to make her change them back" answered Sally leaning forward as she walked close behind him.

"Wha . . what do you mean?" Wesley asked knowing the answer but hoping it wasn't true.

"You know she's a witch, don't you?" said Sally in a matter-of-fact voice.

"No she isn't," answered an alarmed Wesley; more for

the fact that he didn't want it to be true rather than just plain not believing it.

"Yes she is," insisted Sally. "And she likes casting spells on little boys."

"What about Chloe and that new girl then?" argued Wesley.

"Well, she casts spells on girls too, but she prefers boys and there are more boys than girls now since Angelica left" said Sally as if this made it perfectly reasonable to suggest that a boy, and probably a little boy, would be the witch's next victim.

Then, as they turned off the road and onto the path to the old lady's house, Samantha joined in and pointed at a worn-out wooden sign attached the wall of the church yard that read 'No.10 E. Abra'. The seeing that Wesley was close to being convinced, she added, "why do you think her name is Abra?"

"I don't know" answered Wesley, worried that Samantha would tell him.

Which of course she did.

With her eyes as wide as she could manage, she lifted her hands close to Wesley's face and wiggled her fingers.

"It's short for... ABRACADABRAAAAA" she whispered in a way that was just as loud as actually talking.

A panicked Wesley tugged the sleeve of the nearest adult, which happened to be Doctor Clayton, and pleaded, "she's not a witch! . . . Is she?"

"No Wesley, she isn't a witch" said the doctor in an amused, sing-song voice.

"How do you know?" asked Wesley, wanting to believe him.

"Because. . . she's my sister" he answered looking down with a kind smile.

At this, Sally and Samantha looked surprised and embarrassed. They halted for a moment before going on, hoping the doctor would pull ahead of them and not notice that they had called his sister a witch.

"Really, but you don't live here" answered Wesley.

"No, not for a long time now, but I did when I was your age. We both grew up in this very house" the doctor said with an affectionate nod at the house they were now approaching.

This put Wesley at ease, but he was still a little nervous, so asked one last question.

"Then, why is she called Mrs Abacadabra?"

Doctor Clayton laughed at this and reassured Wesley. "It's Mrs Abra, and, hundreds of years ago it used to be Abraham but was shortened. That was her name when she got married. Before that she was Miss Clayton."

Wesley kept a firm hold of Dr Clayton's sleeve as they walked and looked back with a defiant smile at Samantha who was wagging her finger left and right in silent denial of the doctor's explanation.

It was too late, Sally and Samantha's attempt to frighten their little brother had been defeated and Wesley stuck his tongue out at them to show he wasn't scared.

Then, as Wesley turned his head to face forward, he found they had arrived, and standing before him was a beautiful brick house with Mrs Abra already waiting for them in the open doorway.

# CHAPTER 30

# Mrs Abra

Some of the villagers knew Mrs Abra very well and some not so well. The face of the tall lady standing before them had many wrinkles that spread outward in all directions, but instead of making her look old, they just gave the impression of rays of happiness beaming from permanently laughing eyes.

"Oh my what a surprise!" she exclaimed with her left hand over her mouth and, mysteriously, a silver tray of freshly baked goodies in her right hand.

For a moment she just stared at the green, red, blue and gold children before her. Then after a brief glance at her brother Doctor Clayton, she just turned to Mr Saffron who, waving the palm tree he had brought, was first to greet her.

“Hallo Mr Abra. We’ve come for a visit” said Mr Saffron as if half of Cuckoo Village dropping by for tea was an everyday occurrence.

"Hello Mr Saffron, is this for me? Oh thank you, it's a beauty" said Mrs Abra in genuine delight at the sight of the palm he had brought for her.

She stayed in the doorway as the rest of the group arrived. Then, instead of filing into the house, they all fanned out sideways and assembled in a rough semi-circle in front of her.

Then without asking why they'd come she just invited them all in.

"Goodness, what a sight you all are. Come on inside."

"Do you think there's enough room for us all?" asked her brother the doctor.

Although he had grown up in this very house, he hadn't lived in it for many years and couldn't quite remember what extra furniture his sister had for hosting dinners and such. In any case, he didn't think that they had ever had nineteen visitors at once in the house when they were children growing up together.

"Yes, just enough room. Not enough chairs though" she said, wondering for a moment what to do about that.

Mr Saffron filed past her first as she stepped aside to let them all in. He was followed by Mrs Saffron, then Chloe.

"Mrs Saffron" said Mrs Abra.

She didn't say anything else to Mrs Saffron but the way she said her name also said, 'I'm so happy to see you'.

"I do hope you've got the kettle on Mrs Abra I could really do with a cup of your tea" said Mrs Saffron, feeling like she was coming home to see her own mother.

"It is, and you shall have as many cups as you like" Mrs Abra answered with a smile of encouragement.

Then as the golden, glowing Chloe stepped into the house, Mrs Abra looked at her in awe.

"Oh you lucky girl!" she said, to Chloe's surprise.

"Lucky, why?" asked Chloe in wonder at the comment.

Mrs Abra leaned down so her smiling face was close to Chloe's.

"I'll tell you later" she whispered mysteriously.

Then, before Chloe had time to wonder what that meant, Mrs Abra raised the tray of baked goods so it was right under Chloe's nose.

"I just made these, they're still warm. Would you like one?"

The sight of all the delicious goodies on the tray made Chloe instantly forget about Mrs Abra's mysterious comment. She didn't need much time to think though because she spotted her favourite right away. It was a buttered scone, and even though she'd already had one with her breakfast she picked it up quickly but delicately so as not to get her hands messy.

Mrs Abra looked very pleased with Chloe's selection. "That's what I would have chosen" she said.

Chloe then smiled sheepishly and ducked inside.

As soon as he had seen the tray of baked goodies, Oliver pushed his way to the front of the remaining villagers until he was directly behind Chloe.

As he was shorter than Chloe, he had impatiently leaned left and right and raised himself up on his toes to see how Chloe's selection was going to diminish his own choice.

As Chloe had already picked something, Oliver felt more concern about what he wasn't going to get than happiness at having the choice of a piece of cake or a bun in the first place.

Mrs Abra smiled at Oliver as his hand hovered back and forth over the tray of goodies. It wasn't that Oliver couldn't see one that he liked. They all looked delicious, but whatever he chose would mean there would be a baker's dozen or so others that he couldn't have.

He finally grabbed a butterfly bun but walked into the house feeling like he'd just lost twelve or so cakes rather than gained one. And despite loving them, he could never be perfectly happy with a butterfly bun because although they were as sweet as any boy could wish, they were also very light, and this made him feel like he wasn't getting as much.

Mrs Abra's butterfly buns were exceptionally delicious though, so at least for a moment he was content as he raided the centre for the super sweet cream before scoffing the rest down in three quick bites.

The number 10 and also the name E. Abra were ornately carved into the right side of the house doorframe and filled in with gold paint. So, while Oliver took his time to choose, Wesley stood behind him and shyly traced the number and name with his right index finger.

From behind, Samantha leaned in close to him, and this time in a real whisper, she asked "is it made of Gingerbread?"

Wesley looked back and up at her with a slightly scared grin and gave his defiant answer.

"No."

Then hopped onto the doorstep, grabbed a bun without checking which kind or saying hello and darted into the house.

He was followed by Samantha who neither rushed nor dallied so as not to give the very kind old lady any indication that she had called her a witch.

Mrs Abra looked amused at Wesley as he darted past and more so at Samantha as she formally accepted a bun and proud "Thank you" marched inside.

One by one, the rest of the Cuckooers entered the house, grabbing a bun or piece of cake as they filed past. The last person to enter was Doctor Clayton. He ushered Nurse Walton in before him and introduced her to a

Cuckoo villager for the last time that day. He then took the very last item on the tray.

"Looks like we got here just in time" he said with a big smile as he lifted a still warm wedge of chocolate cake to his nose and gave it a long, cheeky sniff.

"You certainly did" answered his sister as she looked back at the strange group milling around in her living room.

She then looked back down to the empty tray she was holding. It didn't make her sad as it might to some people. To a child an empty cake tray means no more desert. To a mother or father, it means there's washing up to do but to Mrs Abra it always meant she could start baking all over again.

She wouldn't start baking just yet though as there were three or four unusual looking neighbours and almost twice as many concerned looking parents in her living room that needed taking care of.

Besides, there were yet more cakes, buns and scones in the kitchen. Better to have too many than not enough was her way of thinking.

CHAPTER 31

# A Very Special Guest

Earlier in the day, something told Mrs Abra that she needed to bake even more than usual. Actually, not something; someone, and it wasn't a person exactly. Well, not a human person.

They didn't know it and neither did Mrs Abra, but the Cuckooers and the four naughty youngling fairies weren't the only ones to visit Mrs Abra that day.

Wiseacre had paid her a visit, and had been whispering in her ear all morning.

Wiseacre had actually been visiting Cuckoo Village. Only it was ten months earlier on an unusually snowy December. He had received a message from his fellow senior fairies about some wayward younglings in the area that were under his care.

That December day, Wiseacre had been working on his own mischievous tricks. One of his specialisations was creating snow and sparkling frost and to add a bit of fun, he had been preparing a snow trap for some unsuspecting humans.

He loved to set just the correct type and amount of snow on the sloped awnings above doors. That way, a slammed door would dump snow onto the door slammer.

Getting the snow to slide off was the easy part, having the human be in just the right spot was the real challenge. Of course, the ultimate goal was to have the snow slide triggered by a sneeze. Fairies were very amused by sneezes and considered it the highest achievement to incorporate a sneeze into their magic.

Wiseacre would chuckle at the thought of all the snow cascading onto people and creating instant snowmen or snowwomen. Or most fun of all, snowboys and snowgirls.

His fun had been interrupted though, and he had to cast a time-travel spell to come ten months forward to September to help sort out the trouble the four younglings were causing.

Wiseacre had decided to make the best of the interruption to his work. So, while he was whispering advice to Mrs Abra, he had also been visiting each of the Cuckoo family homes to observe the goings on. After all, if he was going to be called away from his own mischievous fun to deal with naughty, youngling day-off magic, he might as well enjoy the stories they created.

Now, I don't think I need to explain how it was possible for Wiseacre to take care of Mrs Abra, and also visit each of the Cuckoo family homes all at the same time. After all, you must be an exceptionally bright reader if you found this story, so I'm sure you can work it out for yourself.

Anyway, how senior fairies are able to do the impossible is a more precious secret than how to approach a rainbow without it moving away. So even if I accidentally revealed this secret, I would have been sure to cast a forgetting spell. So, by the time you read this, you would not only have forgotten the secret, but you would have forgotten that you ever knew it.

And now I'm going to have to cast another forgetting spell so that you forget that I told you that you forgot.

CHAPTER 32

# Where to Sit

When Mrs Abra and the doctor followed half of Cuckoo Village into her living room, they were followed by Mirth, Glee, Shimmer, Twinkle and Wiseacre. Of course, the humans couldn't see the fairies, but also Mirth, Glee, Shimmer and Twinkle couldn't see Wiseacre as he watched over them.

Mrs Abra gasped to see her living room so full. The gathering hadn't looked so large as they milled around her front step. Now they were all together inside, it was clear there just wasn't going to be enough room.

Those who knew Mrs Abra well had made themselves at home and were already sitting and those who didn't know her so well were standing, and those children who didn't know her at all were standing half behind them.

Wesley was even behind one of those as he stood very still and observed Mrs Abra closely with an un-chomped slice of cake held low as if he was about to put it in his pocket.

"Oh, not nearly enough chairs" she mused with a soft chicken wing flap of her right elbow into the doctor's side.

Prompted by the elbow jab, Doctor Clayton nodded as he got his sister's meaning in the way that only people who are very close can. In turn, Mrs Abra got his unspoken agreement to her unspoken suggestion as he diverted the use of his mouth from a second chomp on the slice of chocolate cake he had taken to instead say

"Oh, right."

"It's agreed then" declared Mrs Abra. "There isn't enough room 'inside' and it's a nice day so . . . how about we all decamp to the garden and make a picnic of it?"

"Oooo that's a lovely idea!" said a genuinely enthusiastic Mr Sangfroid, who loved picnics almost as much as Mrs Abra and Dr Clayton did.

Then, torn between spending time in Mrs Abra's lovely garden and staying close to all the sandwiches and cakes on the low table in the centre of the living room, he suggested with a longing look at some of the plates "Shall we. . . ?"

In her sing song voice, she declared "Of course, of course. It's not a picnic without something to share."

Mrs Abra strode confidently to the back of the room and pushed open the large French doors which revealed a long, green lawn bordered on both sides by the most splendidly colourful flowering plants. As the doors were flung open, a warm breeze of all kinds of flowery fragrances made its way into the living room. This had a natural but magical effect on the guests, and they all smiled without quite knowing why.

Then she turned and abruptly hefted an armchair out of the way to make room for people to carry the food into the garden.

A few of the adults gasped as, despite being quite old, Mrs Abra easily shifted the heavy looking armchair. In fact, she was as strong and fit as someone very much younger and just as active.

She then scooped up a plate of fairy cakes in her right hand and a basket of fruit in her left, and standing tall said "many hands make light work, everyone grab something and let's get some sunshine."

Then, not waiting for them to follow suit, she marched quickly through open doors and into her back garden.

"Weeeee, a picnic!" sang Twinkle as she flew down and sat on the edge of the plate of fairy cakes that Mrs Abra was transporting to the garden.

"Hello!" said Twinkle to the nearest fairy cake. Then, as her friends joined her, she turned to them and made them giggle with a typical Twinkle joke.

"Hmpfff, not very talkative are they."

"Nor would you be if you were about to be gobbled up by a baby giant" replied Shimmer.

One by one, half of Cuckoo Village's children and adults took a tray of sandwiches, drinks, cakes or other goodies and followed Mrs Abra through the French windows at the back of her house and out into the garden. Doctor Clayton ushered them through, encouraging them not to be shy and he smiled as he looked down to see that the children had their priorities right and had mostly picked up the plates of freshly made cakes and buns.

# CHAPTER 33

# The Picnic

Mrs Abra's back garden was a long, well-tended lawn with all kinds of colourful flower along the sides. The edges of the lawn were not straight, rather, they curved in and out in a way that gave the impression that the colourful flowering plants were pushing forth in waves until the lawn gave way.

Halfway, the lawn had a gentle dip as it rolled down for a way until it flattened out again. And there, stretched out at the bottom of the garden, almost as if it was waiting for them, was a very large, tartan picnic blanket.

"Look!" whispered Sally to Wesley "She used her witchy magic to know we were coming."

Sally hoped to keep Wesley nervous, but it was too late. He already liked Mrs Abra so much that he didn't even care if she was a witch or not.

"Or maybe she has a lot of picnics" he answered without bothering to whisper.

Sally looked disappointed that Wesley was no longer scared of Mrs Abra. Wesley then showed more defiance by walking ahead of Sally and sitting next to the kind old lady before anyone else could take the spot.

Soon, everyone was seated around the edges of the picnic blanket with all the food, drinks, plates and cups spread out on it. The blanket was large, but not quite big enough for all the food and half of Cuckoo Village. So, some sat on the grass at the edges of the blanket, and no one even thought to ask how the grass and the ground below it could be dry so soon after the early morning rain.

Even Mrs Abra didn't think about that and neither did the four youngling fairies. Wiseacre thought about it though. In fact, he had visited the spot earlier that morning to prepare the area and had made sure the ground was dry by casting a perfect picnic spell on it.

After all, picnics are serious business, and it wouldn't do to have them spoiled by wet grass and wet bottoms now would it.

The last person to sit down was Mr Evans. He looked at the ground as if weighing up a challenge. He considered requesting a chair but then imagined how silly he might feel sitting on a throne like a king while everyone sat on the ground around him. So, he accepted the challenge and slowly folded his creaky legs until he was as comfortable as he was going to get.

In fact, it wasn't that comfortable for him as he wasn't used to sitting on the floor, but it was less uncomfortable than not being part of the get-together would have been. It was even less uncomfortable than not being in on the discussion about the goings on of the morning. Most of all, it was less uncomfortable than not having anything interesting to report back to Mrs Evans would have been.

There it was then, sitting on the ground at his age wasn't something his old bones liked, but the company, the conversation and having a story to tell when he got home more than made up for it. And it didn't hurt that there was a delicious feast spread out before him either.

As he took in the sight of the feast laid out before them all, a glint of gold caught his eye. It wasn't Chloe

Saffron as he had become accustomed to her radiant glow surprisingly quickly. The golden glint that had caught his eye was a lovely threading all along the edges of the picnic blanket. He then noticed with wonder that, along with the gold thread, the colours in the blanket's tartan pattern were red, green and blue.

For once, he kept his wonderous observation to himself, but took a long knowing breath through is nose as he puffed out his barrel chest at the discovery. As he exhaled, he slowly nodded in affirmation that today was a truly magical day.

CHAPTER 34

# Butter and Cream

Before long, everyone was chatting in smaller groups as delicious sandwiches, cakes and fruit were being gobbled up and juice and pop was sloshed into plastic beakers and gulped down too.

Thc occasional fly or bee came to see what all the fuss was about before being waved away. A beautiful yellow swallowtail butterfly settled on the top of a bottle of dandilion & burdock for a moment but no one waved it way.

Samantha had already scoffed about as many sandwiches and buns as she could manage, but still reached for a buttered scone. She then turned to David who was sitting beside her.

"Hey David, see if you like butter" she said.

Then before he could answer, she tapped his chin with the scone, so a thick glob of butter stuck to his face.

David grinned in appreciation of the trick as he wiped the butter from the underside of his chin. He first wiped the butter onto the back of his hand then from his hand onto Samantha's arm while the other children laughed, and Mrs Robinson glared at him a little but decided not to tell him off.

Mrs Sangfroid scolded Samantha by telling her to 'behave' in a tone that sounded sing song friendly and menacing at the same time. As she did this, the other adults, including Mr Sangroid, hid their laughing at Samantha's joke by making a pretend disapproval face.

Mrs Abra found the naughty act especially funny but just smiled.

"What? I just saved a buttercup's life" protested the always defiant and cheeky Samantha to her mother.

At this gooey prank, all four fairies rolled around laughing on the almost empty fairy cake plate they were sitting on. Then, strangely, Mirth's invisibility stopped working. As he flickered into view, he immediately took on the look of a firefly. It was only for a moment but the other three stopped laughing in their amazement at this sight as it was something they had never seen before.

Glee, Shimmer and Twinkle were soon back to laughing though as Mrs Robinson, thinking that Mirth was a flitting insect – which is what she was supposed to think, only not at this moment – flicked Mirth away and sent him squishing, face first, into the creamy top of the last fairy cake.

Shimmer and Twinkle quickly flew over to help him. Grabbing a hand each, they pulled with all their might but Mirth was so deeply squished into the fairy cake it was a sticky situation.

Glee could see they were struggling to free Mirth but was unable to help as he was laughing so hard that he could neither fly nor walk.

"Hurry up before someone scoffs me" Mirth laughed despite it being an actual concern.

It wasn't so easy as the fairy cake's cream was very sticky and Glee's wile laughing was becoming infectious.

Eventually, Twinkle placed both feet against the side of the cake and flying horizontally away, she and Shimmer managed to pull Mirth along.

With a long, sluuuurrrp, Mirth oozed free of the thick cream at the top of the cake.

"Oh goodness, thanks for the help Glee" said an exhausted and relieved Shimmer.

"How did it taste Mirthy?" teased Glee ignoring Shimmer's complaint on the grounds that when something is this funny, not helping is entirely justified.

"Quite good actually" replied Mirth cheerfully as he scraped a handful of cream from his face.

Then, "here, try some, see if you like fairies" as he splodged some onto Glee's face.

"Oi, gerrof, that's not butter" he protested as he finally regained his self-control and flew above him laughing.

As the four fairies messed about on the fairy cake plate, the Cuckooers were enjoying Mrs Abra's garden, the unexpected feast and also each other's company so much that they actually forgot why they had come to visit in the first place.

They went through the whole early afternoon picnic lunch without even talking about it. Almost as if it wasn't a concern at all. There was just something about the beautiful garden, the lovely picnic and Mrs Abra's kindness that made them all feel like there was nothing to worry about.

Then, so everyone could hear, Mr Evans swallowed the last bit of his sandwich and coughed loudly and turned to Doctor Clayton and as he did, everyone fell silent in anticipation.

"Well doctor, what's the diagnosis?"

## CHAPTER 35

# The Diagnosis

Doctor Clayton smiled and said "I'm happy to report that the sandwiches and cakes are top notch, and if there are any left, I'd like to take some home?"

Nurse Walton was still biting into a scone, but she knew the doctor was joking because he kindly nudged Vicky, who grinned up at him. Even so, she helped Mr Evan's enquiry.

"And the children?" she asked Mrs Abra as much as the doctor.

At this, everyone looked at Oliver, Max, Vicky and Chloe as if they had just been reminded of something they had completely forgotten about . . . which, they had.

"Oh. . . yeah" said David in realisation as he gave an unconcerned yet curious look at his little brother Oliver.

"Hmmm, well," said the doctor in a more serious tone while mainly addressing the parents.

"We have only done a cursory examination as they would need to come to Plumton for a closer look. But there seems to be nothing physically amiss at all."

"Nothing physically amiss?" said an incredulous Mr Evans.

Everyone looked a little startled by this outburst and seeing this, he realised that he shouldn't worry the children so he smiled and softened his tone.

"They're as colourful as, well, as a jar of Mrs Evans' Rainbow Drops. They looks right at home in Mrs Abra's garden among all the flowers so they do. What do you say to that Mrs Abra?"

At the mention of Rainbow Drops, Mirth stopped wiping fairy cake cream from his hair and looked in surprise at Mr Evans. At first, Shimmer, Twinkle and Glee thought nothing of what was said, but Mirth's sudden attention on Mr Evans focused their own and they got the rainbow connection.

"Ahhhhhh!" said Shimmer.

"Ooo, nice one, someone's paying attention" said Mirth appreciatively.

"Humphhhh" protested Shimmer as she thought Mirth was talking about her taking a moment to realise why Mirth looked pleased with what Mr Evans had said - when he was actually referring to Mr Evans and not Shimmer.

"Sooooo why did it happen?" asked Samantha, looking up to Mrs Abra as if she was sure the old lady must know.

"Well. . . I don't know" answered Mrs Abra shortly.

The adults looked disappointed at this, and the children just looked surprised.

After all the ceremony of marching over here and having an impromptu picnic in the afternoon's autumn sunshine, the children were sure she would know - and some of them even expected her to do a spell to reverse it.

Then she clapped her hands silently together and looked at them all with an expression of wonder on her face like a child with lots of brightly wrapped Christmas presents to open.

"But oh, what a beautiful, colourful sight. How lovely you all look" she beamed.

The entire group, especially the children, all looked a

bit surprised at how much she seemed to like them being unusual colours and not be concerned at all.

"I tried many times but could never catch a rainbow, and now one has popped round for tea!" she proclaimed.

"Ha! She's right, I've also tried to catch one many times but it's impossible," said Mirth testing to see if his forgetting spell worked on his friends.

"Well, we're near one now" answered Twinkle.

"You mean, we 'made' one" replied Shimmer with a giggle.

"Ha, that's what I said" replied Twinkle in a feisty tone as she remembered her great battle with Scintilla earlier that day.

"But what's wrong with them?" asked Sally.

"Oh, there's certainly nothing wrong with them Sally. It's quite the opposite in fact, they're SPLENDID!" she proclaimed.

"But even if there's nothing wrong with them, 'why' did they get . . . rainbowed?" demanded Sally.

After a thoughtful moment, Mrs Abra replied "Well, if I had to guess, I'd say it was magic."

All the adults looked surprised at this, but the children looked delighted.

Then as she paused to look at all their faces as Wiseacre whispered unheard words into her hear, she confidently added, "probably done by mischievous fairies."

## CHAPTER 36

# Rumbled

For once, it was Mirth, Glee, Shimmer and Twinkle's turn to be surprised.

"Heck, we've been rumbled" said Glee with a concerned but excited grin.

"Rumbled? Rumbled?" repeated Twinkle in a panic. She didn't actually know what 'rumbled' meant, or what level of severity being rumbled was, but by the look on Mirth's face it was pretty bad.

"Is being rumbled as bad as being seen?" asked Shimmer to no one in particular.

"We may have been rumbled but we haven't been seen" answered Mirth: more hoping than knowing and forgetting that he had been sploshed into a fairy cake by a human just moments ago. Then, "she doesn't have proof, she's just guessing."

"But how did she know? How did she . . rumble us?" asked Shimmer.

"Either she's had dealings with fairies before or . . . . ." answered Mirth without finishing.

"Or what?" urged Glee as his eyes narrowed with suspicion.

"Or we aren't the only ones playing tricks" replied Mirth.

Mirth had actually been observing Mrs Abra and paying close attention to the extraordinary kindness, love and wisdom that this particular human seemed to have for everyone. He had only seen that before in humans who had a long friendship with senior and very wise fairies; even if they weren't aware of it because the fairy was whispering in their ear in a way that seemed to the human that they were feeling inspired and having their own ideas. Of course, it wasn't exactly the wise fairy that made the human loving and kind but rather it was the human's loving, kind nature that attracted the fairy to them in the first place.

Even Wiseacre was surprised at the old lady's guess of fairy mischief. He was also surprised at Mirth's suspicion that a senior fairy may be guiding of matters. He wondered for a moment if he was failing in his ability to work his magic and guide both humans and youngling fairies without either knowing.

Instead, he concluded that Mrs Abra was an especially wise human and Mirth was an especially bright youngling fairy and that was the reason they were both able to at least suspect there were higher powers at work.

"Rumbled or not, let's see just how much she knows" said Mirth defiantly.

Wiseacre thought that sounded like a good plan, so he borrowed it and thought to himself 'rumbled or not, let see just how much young Mirth knows'.

The five fairies then turned back to Mrs Abra, ever more interested to see how things would play out. Only, instead of sitting in a relaxed way, the four youngling fairies sat at attention and looked like they were ready to scarper in an instant.

## CHAPTER 37

# Wiseacre and Mrs Abra

Wiseacre had known Mrs Abra since she was a little girl, although she had not known him, well, not directly. He was a very old, very clever and, of course, a very wise and senior fairy indeed. He knew some of the highest magic of all. That is, he knew how to make something good come from difficult and challenging situations.

As the four naughty little fairies had caused quite a bit of trouble in Cuckoo Village that day, it was his job to tidy things up. If possible, he preferred to do so in a way that neither the humans nor the naughty youngling fairies were aware of. That way, things seemed to just sort themselves out naturally. That was another part of some of the highest magic; it doesn't seem like magic in the way it is done, but the result is most magical.

A fairy can whisper in a human's ear to guide them, but it usually works better if the human is already of a similar mind and heart to the fairy doing the whispering. This is true whether the fairy is working with a human to do good work or encouraging them to misbehave and cause mischief.

Fortunately, the challenge that Wiseacre faced was made a little easier because of Mrs Abra. The grand old lady was both wise and kind, and that made her a good partner for Wiseacre.

That's also why Mirth had matched himself with

David to help Oliver. David liked mischief too, but he was never cruel and always had an eye on taking care of his younger brothers.

Glee was matched with Max because Glee loved Max's wild and bold nature, but also saw potential in him for kindness.

Shimmer matched with Victoria because Shimmer had a very gentle and kind heart and Victoria had the same even if she needed a little encouragement at first.

Finally, Twinkle matched with Chloe because, although Twinkle is a feisty and even tough fairy at times, once other fairies got to know her, they would always see that she was a very sweet fairy who loves sharing her blessings with others and that's exactly what she intended to encourage Chloe to do.

The more practice fairies have with a particular human, the easier it gets to guide them. So, as Wiseacre was going to be guiding Mrs Abra that day, he felt confident of success because he had known her for many, many years and also liked her very much.

# CHAPTER 38

# Good Old-Fashioned Wisdom

"Magic?" asked Mr Robinson looking down at a very green Oliver.

"And fairies?" added Mrs Sangfroid as she put her arm around Chloe and pulled her a little closer.

"I believe in fairies" said the usually shy and still very golden Chloe.

"Awww" said Shimmer as she softly linked arms with a proudly smiling Twinkle.

Mrs Abra turned a little and gazed deeply into Chloe's eyes. Chloe felt nothing but love and kindness from the old lady, but she looked down and shyly rearranged some of the leftover food on her plate.

Then, looking from Chloe, to Vicky, Oliver and Max and then back again to Chloe, Mrs Abra remembered her promise to tell Chloe why she thought she was lucky.

"When I was little, I would have given anything to be shining gold all over."

"What about green and red and blue" asked Jonathan.

"That too" answered Mrs Abra. Then, laughing, "Or even all at the same time."

Then looking deep in thought, she continued "It seems to me that we wear the clothes that suit our personality. And you may have noticed that the children's overnight . . . transformation, does match their occasional disposition."

"Dispo-what?" asked Samantha.

"Disposition" explained Mr Sangfroid." It means attitude, or, the way you feel."

"So Maxy's red because he's the Dev . . . I mean, because, he, gets angry a lot?" mused Sally.

"No I don't" snapped Max angrily.

A few of the children giggled and Max bit his bottom lip shyly.

"Perhaps" replied Mrs Abra.

"And Oliver is green because he gets car sick" suggested his little brother Jonathan.

"Well, perhaps it's more because he tends to focus a little too much on what others have rather than appreciate what he has himself" said Mrs Robinson as she poked a finger affectionately into Oliver's side.

Oliver squirmed and laughed without realizing that his mother had sweetened her criticism of him with a tickle.

"Aaaaand Chloe is going to be rich one day so she is gold" said Samantha.

"Or because she scoffs too much butter" joked Sally.

"I do like butter but not THAT much" replied Chloe with a grin.

## CHAPTER 39

# Reverse Alchemy

"Oh, Chloe is already rich" explained Mrs Abra. But she didn't explain her meaning because in her life as a teacher she had learned not to just explain everything or give the answers to the students but rather to prompt them to work things out for themselves.

"Really, have you got some treasure Chloe?" asked Oliver.

"Humm, I think it means that Chloe is rich in other things" David said in a way that seems like an opinion but sounds like a question.

"Ah yes!" Mr Robinson said in realisation at the meaning while scuffing David's hair in congratulations. Then he said "Mr & Mrs Saffron love little Chloe to bursting. She's so rich in love she's shining like a little golden Buddah."

“Butter doesn’t shine. Well, only a bit on your chin” said Jonathan.

“Ha, Buddha, not butter dumbo,” teased Sally.

"Eh, so it's a good'un then?" declared Mr Evans. Then, “but surely Mrs Abra, all parents love their little uns. Why aren't they all golden then?”

Mrs Abra liked the blunt way Mr Evans spoke and smiled as she thought for a moment. Then she said "Welllll yes, but love should be passed on rather than stored up like a, ummm."

“Dam!” shouted Jonathan excitedly.

“Heyyyyy!” chastised Mrs Robinson.

“A dam. I mean like a dam. When David made us, I mean when we made a dam on the stream behind our house that time it flooded the back-garden remember?”

“Well I never” said a surprised looking Mr Evans.

“I think the young scamp has it. So, Chloe isn’t shining gold because mom and dad love her so much. It’s because she doesn’t have someone to pass it on to?” he both stated and asked.

“Scamp, hehe,” repeated Oliver with a grin at his younger brother.

Jonathan didn’t mind being called a scamp even though he didn’t know what it meant. He just felt happy to be praised by Mr Evans in front of everyone. He also wondered if it might make his dream of free sweets forever come true.

Then, not wanting Oliver and Max and to feel bad, Mrs Abra clarified. “All emotions are natural. Even anger and, ahm, how shall it put it, concern for resources are good . . . at the right time and proportion.”

The adults pondered this for a moment and the children just didn’t understand so no one replied at first.

Then, Vicky quietly asked "What about me?"

"You’re sad, so you're blue,” said Max.

Max had blurted this out in a direct but insightful way that both impressed everyone and also earned him a quiet 'oi' and a soft nudge from Mrs Sangfroid.

"But that's not bad" said Samantha in encouragement.

Mr and Mrs Sangfroid smiled at Samantha.

Samantha surprised herself with this kindness. It wasn’t that Samantha wasn’t kind, she was actually, it’s just that she was usually so busy teasing people and getting up to all kinds of trouble that people didn't often remember her kind side.

"Your dad's off helping people a lot and you don't know the rest of us that well yet as you only just moved here" added David in support of Samantha's point.

"Yeah, it's normal to be sad when you miss someone. I mean, you're normal. I mean" blundered Sally trying to match Samantha in encouraging Vicky.

Vicky felt a little sadder to be reminded how much she missed her dad, but it also warmed her heart that the other children were supporting her and she briefly smiled at the kind words.

Of course, it wasn't just the other children supporting Vicky, all five fairies had been busy encouraging Samantha, Sally and David to cheer her up.

"We talked about getting Vicky a dog to keep her company but she asked for a brother instead" said Mrs Vauxhall.

"Upgrade" said David triumphantly.

"Downgrade" disagreed Samantha.

At this Sally, Chloe and Vicky laughed and David looked defiant, but the younger boys didn't understand so had no response.

Then it was Jonathan's turn to show kindness to Vicky.

"I want a dog. You can have one of my brothers" he said sincerely meaning it.

"Hey! You're not swapping me for a dog" protested Oliver.

Everyone laughed at Jonathan's cheeky offer of a trade.

Then a very happy looking Wesley surprised even Mrs Abra by gently tugging on her sleeve and asked, “are you an angel?”

The adults smiled and the children looked to see how Mrs Abra would answer and even Mirth, Glee, Shimmer and Twinkle were interested in her answer.

“Oh what a nice thing to be asked. Whatever makes you wonder that” Whatever makes you ask?

“You’re tall and kind and know lots of things. And you’re old” he said.

Then before Mrs Sangfroid could tell him off, he asked “how old ‘are’ you?”

Mrs Abra smiled down at Wesley’s innocent curiosity.

“I’m as old as my tongue and a little older than my teeth.”

She then decided she had said enough and would let the group work things out. And somehow, even without talking much, her wisdom and kindness were inspiring them all. So were the five invisible fairies who presided over them.

After a pause, Mr Evans grew a little impatient at the silence as the discussion had been progressing nicely to that point and he always felt that all the children in Cuckoo Village were like his little nieces and nephews.

"All right, all right. So, Oliver is a bit greed, er envious, Max can be a terror sometimes, little Vicky ere is a bit sad and Chloe’s full of love to bursting. Ding-dong, they wake up green, red, blue and gold one day. Then what's to do? Are they going to stay like that forever? They might as well form a pop-group and call themselves 'The Cuckoo Rainbows.' I'll be their manager and we can do a show in the church hall".

All the children laughed at this. Even Vicky gave a chuckle. The parents appreciated Mr Evans' way of asking for suggestions while encouraging everyone.

"Oi!" declared Mirth. "There he goes again. He's clever that one."

"Is he? Have you seen his shop sign?" laughed Twinkle with a slow shake of her head.

"What? It's clever. It's proportionally and mathematically accurate at least" teased Glee.

At this, the doubly invisible Wiseacre jumped off Mrs Abra's left shoulder, glided over to Sally and whispered a reminder in her ear about something David had once said in class.

Looking thoughtful, Sally said, "once in geography class, Mr Wrigglesworth taught us about some people who were building a railway and he showed us a picture of a big mountain and a valley that was in the way. He asked us how we thought they solved the problem. We had to say, 'they dug a tunnel through the mountain and built a bridge over the valley' but David said 'why don't they just shove the mountain into the valley?' We all laughed but the teacher said it was actually a good idea but the mountain and valley were too far away from each other."

"It WAS a good idea," grinned David still proud of his solution.

"Eh, what's that got to do with anything?" asked Wesley, feeling that he was the boss of Sally and Samantha now they had been shown to be wrong about

Mrs Abra being a witch.

"Well, WESLEY," answered Sally being bossy back to him "Chloe is the mountain and Vicky is the valley."

"What are you on about?" asked Wesley again now even more confused and willing to defend his newfound position of authority.

Nurse Walton looked inspired, impressed and, along with the group, proud of Sally's sudden wisdom and even Sally was a bit surprised at herself.

"So, Chloe has more than enough love and happiness, and Vicky could do with some kindness" she nodded approvingly.

At this, everyone but Mr and Mrs Sangfroid looked approvingly at Chloe and Vicky, but Sally's parents looked on in awe at their usually troublesome daughter.

Sally herself just folded her arms and looked proudly off into the distance as if such wise words were an everyday occurrence with her – which, they definitely were not.

"Chloe dear, why don't you scoot over and sit with Vicky" said Mrs Saffron.

Chloe smiled and was about to shuffle over but Vicky surprised everyone and most of all herself by getting up first and plonking herself down next to Chloe.

Chloe laughed at this abrupt approach. Then turning to her new neighbour, she put her arm around Vicky's shoulders and, talking like a cowboy said "there's gold in them thar hills."

The adults laughed at Chloe's joke and the children laughed without quite understanding it because it just sounded funny.

# CHAPTER 40

# How to Stop a Volcano

"Right then, two down, two to go" said Mr Evans rubbing his hands together enthusiastically.

For some reason, almost everyone looked at Max rather than Oliver.

Max grew uncomfortable at this, like he was going to be blamed for something.

"Wot? I didn't do anything. And I'm not sad" he protested looking at Vicky.

"Or happy" teased Vicky, already starting to come out of her shell.

"Maxy, it's not about right or wrong or good or bad" comforted his dad as he tugged on Max's arm and pulled the lad gently sideways back and forth.

"What about whacking us earlier? That was bad" laughed Sally being her usual disruptive self.

"Watch out or you'll wake up a silly colour, silly sally" shot back Max.

The children all laughed at this.

"What colour's silly?" asked Jonathan.

Nurse Walton coughed slightly to get the groups attention.

"So Max, maybe the next time you feel you are about to get angry at something, you could count to ten first or just try to hold it in and I'm sure with some practice you can control your temper" she said in a gentle tone.

"Ha, good luck. It'll be like trying to cork a volcano"

grinned Samantha.

Max took the challenge and fired back, not too angrily "I can do it silly Sammy."

Glee flew over to Max and hovered invisibly in front of his face. He then looked down at the remaining food on Max's plate and said, "let's see shall we Maxy". He then flew over to Wesley and whispered in his ear.

Suddenly, and completely surprising himself, Wesley leaned forward on all fours and left the safety of Mrs Abra's side. He crawled diagonally to his left across the picnic blanket towards Max, taking care not to upset any of the plates.

When he got just beyond striking distance from a bemused looking Max, he slowly reached out his hand and picked up the slice of chocolate cake that was on Max's plate. Then, before any objection could be made, and all the time keeping eye contact with Max, he stuffed the slice into his mouth even though there wasn't room for it all.

Max looked shocked and as his eyes bulged in outrage, he seemed to turn an even deeper shade of red for a moment.

Everyone else at the picnic was shocked too; as much by Wesley's bravery as the actual cake raid. Even Mr and Mrs Sangfroid were too stunned to admonish Wesley.

Wesley pushed so hard to feed the rest of the fat wedge of chocolate cake into his mouth that the cream in the middle started to ooze between his fingers.,

All the fairies, including Wiseacre were just as surprised at Wesley's actions as the humans. But when Mirth and Glee saw chocolate cream oozing between his fingers and dripping onto the picnic blanket, they laughed loudly and shimmer and Twinkle hid their amusement in mock disgust.

Wesley started slowly backing up the way he had come. His retreat was hindered by the fact that doggy walking backwards on only two knees and one hand wasn't as easy as going forwards on all fours.

As Wesley backed away, he maintained eye contact with Max as if this was his only protection against a sudden whopping.

Everyone remained silent as they were over their shock and eager to see what would happen. The only sound, apart from Wesley clinking the occasional plate with his knees or feet as he backed away, was a very short 'oh' from Jonathan as he caught himself from letting out an excited whoop at the tension.

As volcanic anger built up within him, Max continued to glare at the slowly retreating Wesley. As Wesley reached the halfway point back to safety at Mrs Abra's side, he had wolfed enough of the cake down to be able to speak in a very muffled way.

Wesley meant to say 'you don't mind if I have this do you Maxy?' in the most unaware, innocent way. But it came out of his nearly full mouth as "Yer dn't mnd ff ah" gulp "av thiz der yer Maxy?"

Wesley then quickened his pace as his fourth paw was free to aid him in his effort to back away. As he put distance between himself and the volcano, he showed consideration for poor Mrs Abra's picnic blanket by using the relatively clean knuckles of a chocolate squelched fist instead of the gunked palm of his hand to walk on.

Just about everyone present expected Max to launch

himself at Wesley in response to the outrage, and Mr Sangfroid slowly put his orange juice down so he could be ready to grab Max's ankle mid-flight if he sprang into action.

Max felt the whole gathering waiting in expectation and now it was time for him to surprise himself and everyone else.

Although his anger at Wesley stealing his cake grew and grew, he still wasn't done with his anger at Sally for doubting his ability to control himself and he wanted to punish her. So, he prioritised his revenge and gritted his teeth as he answered "nope". He then cleared his throat a little and continued in a strained tone "you can have it."

Max's words were not kindly or patient, but most of the children could hardly believe what they were hearing. All the adults and some of the children, Wesley most of all, looked delighted at Max's effort in self-control.

Sally and a few of the other children were disappointed that there wouldn't be a scrap. Samantha screwed up her face as it was now twice in one day that the terrible twosome hadn't been able to stir up trouble.

Of course, what almost everyone, apart from Mrs Abra, didn't understand about the miracle was that Max hadn't suddenly turned into a saint. He hadn't even stopped being angry. Instead, he had listened to their conversation about him. He had also listened to Glee who had whispered in his ear encouraging him to learn self-control.

Glee had simply whispered "be angry with your anger."

So Max was still as angry as ever and he was still acting on his emotions, but he had decided to control and focus them rather than having his anger control him.

For the first time, Max had begun to see his anger as an outside force, an invader taking control of him, and he didn't much like that. So, he decided to put up a fight with the invader and see if he could resist it.

Max still liked getting angry but had decided from that moment that he would direct his anger and not let his anger direct him. So, as an experiment, he decided to do nothing just to see who was boss. He also wanted to show Sally that she was wrong and it's always nice when you can achieve two things at once isn't it?

Inside, Max was angry about Wesley stealing the slice of chocolate cake he had been looking forward to scoffing. He was also pretty sure that Wesley deserved a good whopping for the crime. However, at that moment, he had more important battles to wage. For the first time that he could think of, Max had wrestled with his anger. . . and won.

Glee's eyes went wide, and as he puffed out his chest, he covered his upper lip with his lower lip.

"Good boy Maxy" congratulated Glee as Mirth, Shimmer and Twinkle clapped in delight and congratulated Glee in turn.

"Very well-done Glee!" all three of his friends called out excitedly.

So did Wiseacre who was very pleased with the result of Glee's effort, though no one could hear him.

"Well, it really is a day for magic and miracles!" exclaimed Mr Evans. Then, looking at Max "I do believe Max looks a little less red than before. No, I'm sure of it."

The others considered this, some tipping their head to

the side a little as the doctor had done to his patients, as they observed Max.

"You know I think you're right Mr Evans. Well done Max," said Mrs Sangfroid.

Max felt proud of himself and a little shy at getting so much attention and congratulations. Although as he was becoming a less red due to his efforts at self-control, he began to blush and his face became naturally more red.

"Nope, he's redder again" giggled Samantha.

"Aw, he's blushing. So cute!" said Mrs Robinson.

Max was more used to being told to calm down or to stop whopping people. Being praised made him feel funny inside. As the happy emotion bloomed within his heart, there was less and less room for his anger and soon he wasn't angry at all.

Then as a final reward, Mrs Sangfroid took one of the last two slices of Victoria Sponge Cake from a cake plate and put it on Max's now empty plate and gave him a pat on the head.

# CHAPTER 41

# Higher Magic

Mrs Sangfroid turned to Mrs Abra and asked, "so if the children's . . . 'illumination' is a reflection of their state of mind then is adjusting their state of mind the way to reverse the, er, spell or magic or whatever did it to them?"

Mrs Abra answered, "we may never know what magic some naughty little fairies used to play this trick on the children. But whatever it was, it would be what I like to call 'elemental magic'. The magic of nature. But there are other kinds of magic, higher kinds. Magic that is so wonderful that we don't even know it's magic.

"Like what" interrupted Oliver.

Mrs Abra turned to Oliver and addressed him directly with a warm smile which made him feel both happy and shy. She was well practiced in loving children and also teaching them as she had children of her own and now had grandchildren and had also worked her whole life as a teacher at Plumton Elementary and Middle School.

"Well Oliver, elemental magic can create, or change things such as all the beauty in nature. The clouds, the rain, the grass we sit on, flowers and the trees and the stream over there along with the fish swimming in it. It creates all the animals and birds and even us.

Is it their job? asked Jonathan.

Mrs Abra smiled at this and answered "those who do the magic, get to enjoy the beauty they create. It's like food for them. The most nutritious and delicious of all is when fairies get to experience human appreciation for the beauty they create. They work very hard to create the beauty we see all around us, and when they experience our joy, they feel energized."

"I thought everything is created by God?" challenged Samantha.

Samantha was still hoping to convince Wesley that Mrs Abra was a witch even though she didn't believe it herself.

Mrs Abra knew what Samantha was up to and it delighted her to play the game.

"And so it is Samantha, but even the greatest of creators uses tools and helpers."

"Like angels?" asked Wesle.

"Mmm that's right" she replied looking down at him and patting him on the shoulder.

"And fairies?" asked Sally.

"And fairies" confirmed Mrs Abra. Then, "yes, I believe so."

"Rumbled" said a nervous Twinkle.

"So why did these naughty fairies only magic some of us?" asked Chloe.

The question was directed at Mrs Abra but the old lady had learned from her days as a school teacher to give students a chance to work things out for themselves. Instead of answering, she looked around and settled her gaze on Nurse Walton.

Nurse Walton was a little surprised to be expected to answer that on. After thinking for a moment, she observed "well, not all the children got . . . magicked but one child from each family with children in the village did."

Then Doctor Clayton added "and I supposed you could say that some lessons are learned through direct experience and some through indirect experience. So, in a way, all the children are learning something today."

"And the adults" added Sally.

"Ohhh for sure, the adults too" agreed Mr Evans with a toothy grin.

## CHAPTER 42

# The First is Last

Now that the group had discussed Chloe, Victoria and Max, everyone was in anticipation as to what would be said about Oliver. As no one said anything on the matter, Oliver's little brother Jonathan decided to help out.

"So Oliver, you're green so stop being greedy and jealous" blurted out Jonathan as he wagged his toastless finger at his green older brother.

At the bluntness of this, all four young fairies and all the children laughed out loud.

"Jonyyyy!" protested Mrs Robinson.

"No I'm NOT," came the predictable reply from Oliver.

Oliver meant it, but struggled not to laugh.

"Have you looked in a mirror recently Oli?" called out David.

"I'm not jealous am I mum?" protested Oliver as he tugged on his mother's sleeve.

"Well, not 'jealous', but you are a little prone to envy?" suggested his mother in a comforting tone.

"What's the difference?" asked Vicky who had a talent for language and loved to learn new words and their meanings.

At this, some of the adults weren't sure how to explain and weren't even sure they knew themselves.

"They are often the same, but sometimes jealous is when you don't like someone else taking something that is yours. And envy is when you want something that belongs to someone else" said Mr Evans in a friendly tone.

Vicky thought for a moment then offered an example.

"So, if Jonathan took Oli's bike and rode it to the shop, Oli might be jealous. And if Jonathan bought some sweets then Oli might be envious" she said, almost to herself so as to check if she understood what Mr Evans had said.

"There's no 'might' about it," laughed Sally.

"Good example Vicky" congratulated Mr Evans.

"So, you have to let me ride your bike and you can't have any of my sweets. Then you'll get better" said Jonathan happy to help.

Oliver breathed in deeply and sighed a long "Okayyyyy" to his little brother.

Getting into a helpful spirit herself, Samantha reached out and took the last slice of Victoria Sponge Cake and put it on her plate. Then, lifting her plate to her nose, she sniffed the slice deeply while looking at Oliver with a blissful expression. When she was sure he was looking back, she let out a long, taunting "Hmmmm so delicious."

At this, Oliver suddenly got a strong desire for some Victoria Sponge Cake and licked his lips a little. Then he looked down at the empty plate and started to panic.

Mirth quickly flew over to Oliver and whispered encouragement into his ear to counter Samantha's attack.

At that moment, Oliver remembered the great effort Max had made to control himself and wanted to follow his example.

"Enjoy . . ." said Oliver generously.

Samantha teased back “I will” and took a huge bite adding through a full mouth “soooo good.”

Then Oliver’s eyes narrowed a little and finishing his sentence, he sprung his trap “. . . your Turkish Delight.”

Samantha froze and looked left and right confused for a moment. Then there was a flash of recognition and her eyes involuntarily darted to Mrs Abra then back again to Oliver.

She raised a cupped right hand to her chin as if she was going to spit the cake out but instead, she just chewed a bit slower. Then with a reluctant gulp, she swallowed and slowly put the plate down as if she was unconcerned but in no hurry to finish.

Mrs Abra laughed out loud at this and complimented Oliver.

“Oh well done Oliver” she said softly clapping her hands together.

It wasn’t clear if she was praising Oliver for his effort in self-control or his clever tease at Samantha. Oliver didn’t care which as he just enjoyed winning in his exchange with Samantha and being praised for it was a bonus.

“Oooo I’m so proud my little green apple” said Mrs Robinson giving Oliver a squeeze and an enthusiastic pinch on the cheek that hurt him a bit.

“Owww” protested Oliver happily.

# CHAPTER 43

# Is that It?

Everyone seemed satisfied that the matter of the totally, completely green, red, blue and gold children was resolved. Even though they remained totally, completely green, red, blue and gold.

Before long, everyone was back to chatting in smaller groups until Sally piped up.

"Is that's it? she said in disappointment.

"They get zapped into rainbow colours by bad fairies and have to behave themselves back again by being good."

"Oi, we're not bad" shouted an annoyed Twinkle even though Sally couldn't hear her.

"Well, if it was indeed the work of fairies, let's say it was fairies' mischievous way of being helpful rather than bad" replied Mrs Abra.

"That's better" said Shimmer nodding along with Twinkle.

"I mean, can't somebody do some magic back at them" replied Sally not making it clear if she meant to change the children back or to get revenge on the fairies.

"That's a fair question" said Wiseacre to himself as neither human nor fairy could hear him. At least no fairy junior to him.

"And who would that someone be exactly?" asked Doctor Clayton trying hard not to laugh.

"Well, I don't know," answered Sally looking down and playing with her half-filled plastic cup of orange juice.

Mrs Saffron nodded her head thoughtfully and said "I think . . . the higher magic Mrs Abra talked about is being done right here isn't it? We all come together as one Cuckoo family and the magic of love and wisdom is helping, isn't it?"

"What could be more magical?" agreed Mr Saffron as he looked lovingly at his wife and little golden daughter.

"Hmphh, looping a rainbow for a start" said Glee as his three friends nodded in agreement.

"We have our magic and they have theirs," said Mirth.

"Well, I think it's been a most magical day and there's no harm to the children it seems. Right doctor?" added Mr Robinson.

Doctor Clayton and Nurse Walton both nodded agreement to this.

"And we got a jolly good picnic out of it too" added Mr Evans still stuffing his face.

"We'll come back in a few days and check in on the children but if it isn't my imagination, they have all started to change hue already" encouraged the doctor.

Everyone looked at the four rainbow children and seemed to agree that they were still definitely green, red, blue and gold, but not totally, completely.

It seemed settled and everyone felt that everything was going to just fine. Even though four of their children were still green, red, blue and gold from head to toe.

It was just that, no one seemed too concerned about it. Not even the children themselves.

CHAPTER 44

# Story Time

esley looked up at Mrs Abra and tapped her gently on the arm.

"You said you used to have picnics and tell stories when you were little didn't you?" he enquired.

"Yes, I did indeed, right on this spot. And also, when I was big, with my own children. And now I'm having a picnic with you" replied Mrs Abra smiling back at Wesley.

"Can you tell us one now then?" Wesley asked.

"Well," replied Mrs Abra looking around to see if the others would like to hear a story.

"Oh yes, I'd like to hear one" said Chloe with her arm still around Victoria's shoulders.

"Me too" nodded Victoria.

"Us too" squeaked Shimmer and Twinkle as if the whole group could hear them.

All of the other children agreed, and even the adults looked hopeful.

"It's been quite a while so I'd love to hear one too. I've been telling Nurse Walton about your famous stories and poems for years now and I think she's wondering if I made it all up" said her younger brother.

Nurse Walton smiled at this.

"Perhaps Mrs Abra will tell us a story if the little ones promise to help clear all the plates and things after we finish the picnic" said Mr Robinson as much to Mrs Abra as to the children.

All the children nodded enthusiastic agreement to this.

Mrs Abra was happy to tell her guests a story but she felt sure that Nurse Walton must know some good poems and stories too and thought it was a good opportunity for her to get closer to the Cuckoo children as well as the parents.

"Well, I like to hear poems, songs and stories too" teased Mrs Abra.

Then, looking around the picnic blanket and settling her gaze on Nurse Walton, she added "I'm sure you know some good one's don't you Jenny?"

For some reason, being called Jenny by Mrs Abra made her feel like a little girl in school again and this caused her to laugh out loud.

"Me, oh" she replied while she gathered her thoughts.

Glee clapped his hands together and rubbed them like he was about to conjure some kind of spell.

"Oooo goody" he said.

Then he flew down and rested on Max's right shoulder and made himself comfortable.

Mirth was already perched on Oliver's shoulder and called over to Glee.

"Let's see if humans are any good at telling stories."

"I've got a feeling this one will be" Glee replied.

Glee meant Mrs Abra as Nurse Walton hadn't agreed to tell the children a story or recite a poem yet.

In anticipation of story time, Shimmer and Twinkle both sat at the midway point on Chloe's left arm which was still around Victoria's shoulders, and all four girls, Shimmer & Twinkle and Chloe & Victoria waited in excitement for the story to begin.

## CHAPTER 45

# Jenny's Turn

A somewhat nervous Nurse Walton looked around at all the Cuckooers sitting on the picnic blanket until her eyes eventually rested on Mrs Abra. When she felt the kind old lady's gaze still upon her she didn't feel nervous any longer.

"Very well" she smiled.

Nurse Walton wondered for a moment what story she might tell. She noticed a bee hum towards the picnickers to have a quick look over the group. she remembered a poem she and her brothers used to recite to make each other laugh when they were children.

Nurse Walton's face lit up as she prepared to recite the poem.

"This poem is called 'The Race'" she said in a wonderous tone that caused some of the children and a couple of fairies to squirm in excitement.

### The Race

*A bee, a boy, a bug and a bunny*
*all had race because they thought it would be funny.*
*The bee was doing well until it spotted a flower.*
*The boy was running fast until he ran out of power.*
*The bug was winning but was squished by the bunny.*
*The bunny couldn't run because he thought it was so funny.*
*A bee, a boy, a bug and a bunny*
*all had race because they thought it would be funny.*
*Nobody finished, so nobody won.*
*But everyone, except the bug, had fun.*

As she concluded the poem everyone clapped and also laughed at the silly ending.

“Ha ha, oh the poor bug” laughed Shimmer along with Twinkle and along with Vicky and Chloe.

“Har, that’s pretty good, what do you think Glee” said Mirth.

“I think I have some competition,” said a smiling Glee who was well known as best composer of songs and poems among all the fairies.

“So who was fastest?” asked Jonathan.

“It was the bee wasn’t it? Bees can go faster than people and rabbits, can’t they?” said Oliver.

“Well, none of them won but it does seem the bee was in the lead” said an amused Mr Evans now also wondering which could go faster.

“Did the bug die?” asked Jonathan looking concerned.

“They’re not real” spoiled Sally shaking her head slightly as she said the word ‘real’.

“No, I think it went to the vet and got fixed” said Mr Sangfroid as a way of making up for Sally’s tease.

“Well, it was a very nice poem, Nurse Walton. Thank you” said Mrs Vauxhall as the others nodded their agreement.

“Now it’s your turn” said Wesley smiling up at Mrs Abra.

# CHAPTER 46

# Smiling Faces

Mrs Abra enjoyed Nurse Walton's poem very much and made a note to remember it so she could tell it someday.

Then, looking over the splendid sight of all her visitors, she decided on a poem that she thought would fit the occasion.

"Well, this is a silly poem I made up when I was little. I used to tell it to my little brother, but he always seemed to forget it, so I got to tell it to him many times. That's probably why I memorised it so well even if he didn't."

"One of the perks of having a poor memory is that you get to enjoy stories like they are new every time" said her younger brother Doctor Clayton.

"Ok here goes then. It's about a little boy who can't seem to smile anymore. So, his sister tries to help him" said Mrs Abra introducing the poem.

"And it's called 'Tommy had a broken smile'," she announced dramatically as the group settled down again.

Tommy had a Broken Smile

*Tommy had a broken smile*
*It didn't seem to work.*
*I told him jokes for a while,*
*but he couldn't even smirk.*

*The two of us then in we go,*
*to say hello to dad.*
*And even though Tom loved him so,*
*he still looked awfully sad.*

At being reminded of how much she missed her own father, Vicky looked sadder, and in fact, a little bluer again. Then she felt a little better when Chloe noticed this and gave her shoulder a squeeze. As she did this, Chloe become a little less radiantly gold and Vicky became a lighter shade of blue.

*Dad wondered what could be amiss,*
*so, he called out to mum,*
*who tried to fix things with a kiss,*
*yet still Tom's face was glum.*

*We visited our friend the clown,*
*whose name is Mr Snuckle.*
*But he just made Tommy frown,*
*although, he made me chuckle.*

*The doctor we next went to see,*
*who'd known Tom since birth.*
*But in him could find no glee,*
*nor any trace of mirth.*

"Heyyyy" said Mirth looking at Glee with a combination of wonder, surprise and suspicion. "We're in it!"

"How could our names be in it when it's from before

we even existed?" asked Glee looking as surprised as could be.

"Maybe it's just a coincidence" said Shimmer, raising her hands with a dismissive shrug of her shoulders.

"Yeah, anyway, the doctor couldn't find Glee and Mirth because you are invisible. Now shhhh sillies, I can't hear" complained Twinkle.

Mrs Abra was going on with the poem and Mirth and Glee also wanted to hear the rest, so they kept quiet while demonstrating with their faces that it wasn't because the girls told them to.

*Our little group took Tom to town,*
*to cheer him with ice-cream.*
*Yet after he had wolfed it down,*
*he still refused to beam.*

*Then we all pondered him*
*and tried to figure out,*
*what could give his face a grin,*
*to replace the pout.*

"Who's there?" interrupted Jonathan "did they all go, even Mr Snuckle?"

"Yes, so far, Tommy, his sister, Mum & Dad, Mr Snuckle and the doctor" said David with a look of pride on his face that he remembered everyone.

"Show off" whispered Samantha.

"Did everybody get ice cream" asked Oliver.

"Yesssss Oliver, everybody got some" added Sally with a slight shake of her head and roll of her eyes.

Mrs Abra continued with the poem.

*The ice-cream man then inquired,*
*whom Tom wished to see?*
*Some of us guessed he desired*
*to visit Uncle Lee.*

*Lee tried to do what I had done,*
*and we laughed at his jest.*
*But Tom could not enjoy the fun,*
*and showed no sign of zest.*

"Zessst hehe" giggled Wesley. He always tried out funny sounding words. His parents and teachers weren't sure if that meant he would have a talent for language, music or both.

"What's zest?" Max asked.

"It means having lots and lots of fresh, positive energy" explained Mrs Abra.

"Oh" answered Max nodding a few times then holding his eyebrows raised to show that he was waiting for her to continue with the poem.

She did so.

*Uncle Lee now looked bemused,*
*and said 'there's but one place,*
*where nephew Tom would be amused*
*and have a happy face'.*

*Grandparents Smith, and also Jones,*
*lived right here in town.*
*If Tom could visit both their homes*
*he might not feel so down.*

*Four smiling faces, old and wrinkled,*
*though within they glimmered.*
*Eight loving eyes that all twinkled*
*and so brightly shimmered.*

"Oi, now it's us," squeaked Shimmer and Twinkle at the same time.

"Ha ha yeah, old and wrinkled" shouted Glee laughing from across the picnic blanket.

"Hey that's not what I mean" Twinkle shouted back.

"And you're older than us" added Shimmer.

"Excuse me, can we hear the story please" complained Mirth in vengeful tease.

"Fine" came back Shimmer's defiant reply as she turned back to Twinkle in wonder, and they giggled to one another in delight at making it into Mrs Abra's story.

*They looked surprised at such a crowd*
*coming to their door.*
*We had tea and scones and talked so loud,*
*and then they gave us more.*

*We all were having so much fun,*
*we near forgot the lad.*
*When they asked us why we'd come,*
*we told them Tom was sad.*

*'Whatever do you mean they said,*
*he grins from ear to ear'.*
*And when we turned and saw his head*
*it had a naughty leer.*

*Little Tommy looked so pleased.*
*He'd played the greatest trick.*
*He had fooled us with his tease,*
*pretending to be sick.*

*Now Tommy had such a smile,*
*and sometimes a grin.*
*He had tricked us for a while,*
*and we all said, 'you win'.*

*Then we asked him, 'please be fair,*
*Why did you make us fall*
*for your trick?' and he declared*
*'Because I MISSED YOU ALLLL!'*

As the poem ended, everyone was silent for a moment. That usually means people didn't like something or they really, really liked it.

Then, all together, everyone clapped enthusiastically and said how much they loved the story, and this made Mrs Abra very happy.

"It's like us isn't it?" said Chloe with her face glowing with golden light at happiness from hearing the story.

"A bit, but not exactly. And I made this up a long before you were born" replied Mrs Abra.

"Is Tommy Vicky then?" asked Max in his usual blunt way.

"No because Vicky is a girl . . . and, she's called Vicky" answered Samantha quickly, more to defeat Max than to defend Vicky.

Max would usually take the bait and shout an angry reply at Samantha but he had determined to win by trying to not allow himself be controlled either directly by his feelings or indirectly by someone teasing him. At least for the rest of the day.

At this, Samantha saw Max suddenly become less red and she felt disappointed that he didn't react but also proud of her little brother for doing well.

"And Tommy wasn't really sad, he was just pretending to trick them all into giving him ice cream" added Sally with appreciative smile.

"I think he wanted to get all his friends together and the ice-cream was a bonus" corrected David.

"Know it all" shot back Sally preferring her version.

Mrs Abra looked delighted that the children were discussing her poem. She always saw this as a sign that it was a good story.

"So is Vicky just pretending to be sad to get cakes" asked Oliver more in admiration than curiosity and also thinking about giving it a try sometime.

Vicky found this funny and laughed as she denied it. "Noooooooo."

"I think Vicky is naturally sad because her dad works away so much. Wouldn't you be Oli?" said Nurse Walton in a way that encouraged both Oliver and Victoria.

"I still like the cakes though" said Vicky with a smile.

# CHAPTER 47

# Maybel's Visit

Suddenly, Vicky stopped smiling and turned with everyone else to look beyond the stream that ran past the bottom of Mrs Abra's garden.

Their attention was caught by a loud, inquisitive 'mooooo' from Maybel, one of Farmer Crabtree's cows. Maybel had munched her way to the bottom of the cow field as she chomped at some of the last of the dandelions which were her favourite desert.

Maybel was about to gobble the very last dandelion when she noticed the goings on across the stream. Looking up, she had given them a long 'what's going on' moooo.

The children laughed at Maybel's curious mooing and soon enough heard a bark from Farmer Crabtrees dog Nuzzler as she darted their way. Nuzzler was followed a way back by Farmer Crabtree.

Farmer Crabtree wasn't worried about Maybel sploshing through the stream and attempting to gobble up Mrs Abra's picnic. He knew that his cows always kept to their side of the stream. But he did want to make sure she didn't head off into the woods. She would sometimes get stuck in there on an occasional greedy hunt for more dandelions to gobble up.

Maybel was snuffling around in the grass at the bottom of the field looking for more dandelions to scoff but she couldn't find any, so she settled for munching at the grass.

"Take her back up lass" called out Farmer Crabtree.

At this Nuzzler ducked her head all the way down to the ground and eyed Maybel up, then she loped away as she dipped left and right. Then with a bark, circled around between Maybel and the stream.

Maybel looked annoyed at having her munching disturbed. She was sure there must be more dandelions around somewhere but didn't much like Nuzzler pestering her while she ate.

In a huff, she snuffled loudly then, with one final, disappointed look around, she reared away and headed back up the field towards the rest of the herd. She made sure to walk slowly just to shoe Nuzzler that she wasn't the boss of her.

Nuzzler followed her closely, all the time ducking to the left and right to make sure Maybel didn't turn back again.

As Maybel and Nuzzler passed Farmer Crabtree, he gave his favourite cow a pat on the side and nodded his faithful working dog on with an enthusiastic "goo on lass."

Instead of following them, he continued walking towards the stream to say hello the picnickers.

When he drew close enough to see who was who at the gathering, he called out with his usual greeting.

"Now then". He said.

The picnickers all looked back at the rosy cheeked farmer greeting them from across the stream as if they had been caught doing something they shouldn't. They wondered how he would react to seeing such a large picnic with a few of the children looking so unusual –

and on a school day too.

"Ho hoh!" he called out cheerfully at the sight of the group.

"Avin a pantomime picnic are you Mrs Abra?" he enquired.

Then "I do ope you ave some of Mrs Crabtree's butter on them scones."

"We do, and there's plenty of them so you are welcome to come over and have one if you can find a path across Mr Crabtree" replied Mrs Abra looking genuinely happy to see him.

"Oh I'd love to Mrs Abra, but Mrs Crabtree would ave my ide if I spoiled my appetite before dinner" he laughed.

At this, Mr Evans thought about Mrs Evans preparing his dinner and thought better about stuffing another piece of cake into his mouth and slowly put it back on the cake plate.

With a last look at the colourful children and a shake of his head, the rosy cheeked farmer gave a casual wave goodbye as he turned and headed back up the field. Then with his back to them he called out.

"Cheerio. Enjoy your picnic. I'll make sure ole Maybel doesn't come and scoff any of it."

Then, with a single bark, he was greeted by Nuzzler who had completed her task of returning Maybel to the herd and had rushed back to be by his side again.

CHAPTER 48

# Picnic's End

The short visit from Maybel, Nuzzler and Farmer Crabtree seemed to be a sign that the picnic was coming to an end.

Along with most of the group, Doctor Clayton would have rather stayed for the whole rest of the day. He first looked up at the sun and noticed it was already getting low in the sky. Then he confirmed the late hour with a quick look at his watch.

"Well, I think it's time we were on our way back to Plumton Nurse Walton. What do you say?" he said.

Nurse Walton reluctantly agreed, brushed some grass and cake crumbs from her lap then, along with the doctor and some of the parents, stood up.

"Wait, Johnny, did you bring your camera" asked Sally because she knew he took it almost everywhere.

"Yeah, can we take a picture?" asked Jonathan.

"That's a wonderful idea" said Mr Robinson. Then "That is, if you don't mind 'the' children being photographed" he said, nodding towards Chloe and Vicky.

"Oh that would be lovely. Wouldn't it Vicky?" said Mrs Vauxhall.

Vicky and Chloe both nodded enthusiastically.

"Everyone gather round then" said Mr Robinson as he ushered his family to the other side of the picnic blanket where Mrs Abra was now standing alongside the doctor and Nurse Walton who was puling on Mr Evan's elbow to help him up.

"Who's going to take the picture? If Jonny takes it, he won't be in it" asked Wesley.

"It has a timer" grinned Jonathan.

Jonathan then set his camera up on a nearby bird table. The post holding up the table was quite old and leaning to one side so the camera wasn't level. He looked on the ground and found a few stones then tried different sizes under one side of the camera until he found one that was just the right size to keep it level.

After Jonathan set the timer on the camera to ten seconds, he rushed back to the group where Mr Evans was bossing everyone around to get them in order.

"Right ho, the adults at the back, the elder children in the middle and the little uns at the front" he fussed.

Without being told to do so, Oliver, Vicky, Chloe and finally Max sat on the grass close to one another at the centre of the group.

"Ooo I've never had my picture taken. Let's get in," said Shimmer as she hovered in front of Victoria.

"But we won't be in it, will we?" asked a worried Twinkle looking at Mirth.

Mirth reassured them, "when the humans see the picture, they will see fireflies but when fairies see it, they can see us."

Glee teased the girls with a slow shake of his head "Eeeeveryone knows thaaaaat."

"They do now," laughed Shimmer.

Twinkle then flew into the group and likewise, hovered in front of Chloe. Mirth perched on Oliver's right shoulder sitting with his arms folded looking proud of himself and Glee stood on Max's head in triumph with his arms in the air.

As they waited for the camera's timer to run down and take the picture, Mr Evans shouted with a booming, joyful voice, "everyone say butterrrrrr!"

At this, the whole group laughed then complied and shouted a long, drawn out "butterrrrrrrrrrr!" Then, with a crisp 'click,' the picture was taken.

As Jonathan retrieved his camera from the bird table, the rest of the group settled into smaller groups and stood around the picnic blanket chatting away just as they had when they were first sitting in the same spot.

As the parents started to say their goodbyes, the children talked and played around them until Mr Evans gave a loud yet hesitant cough and both of his eyebrows too charge of matters as they pointed at the plates and cups until some of the children got their meaning.

"Oh yeah" said Chloe remembering their promise. Then she reached down and started to stack empty plates on top of each other.

Vicky also took some plates with cakes and buns still on them and moved them all to one plate then put empty plates under to make them easier to carry.

David joined in, and with a nod and a soft elbow push from some of their parents, the rest of the children started to help too. As they did, the parents and the rest of the adults all smiled looked very happy to see the children helping to clear the plates and cups.

As the children continued discussing Mrs Abra's story, the autumn sun was moving further towards the horizon in the west. The shadows cast by the plants and trees were getting longer and this was a sure sign to the fairies that it was almost time for them to go home too.

CHAPTER 49

# Goodbyes

As the Cuckooers cleared away the picnic or chatted in the garden, Mirth, Glee, Shimmer and Twinkle gathered together and sat on the edge of the bird table that Jonathan had used for his camera. Swinging their legs back and forth, they looked on at the group in front of them.

"I like this lady, she's almost as good as Glee at stories. I'm going to visit her again to listen to more" said Mirth.

"Hmmm me too. It was pretty good, specially the part where we are in it" agreed Glee.

“Oh” cooed Twinkle, “the lady said that when she was little, she used to go on picnics with her brother and tell lots of stories. I wish I could go back and enjoy them.”

“Fairies don’t make wishes Twinks, they grant them” teased Glee with a grin.

Shimmer jumped to Twinkles defence by giving Glee a shove.

“Hey Mirth, didn’t you once tell us that some fairies can travel back and even forwards in time? Well, why can’t we go back to when Mrs Abra was little? I want to hear the stories too” said Shimmer.

“Yeah, rewind the movie, I missed the first part laughed” Twinkle.

“Well, I once heard it said but I’m not sure I believe it,” replied Mirth with a serious and thoughtful look. Then he added “but don’t worry, I’m already looking into it."

Mirths friends smiled as they knew if there was a secret of how to travel back in time, then Mirth would eventually find it once he had made up his mind to look for it.

For a while, the four fairy friends turned their conversation to their adventures with their children. Listening in wonder at the stories each told of their funny and beautiful experiences.

It really had been a day of stories, of hearing, telling and even making them. As far as a youngling fairy was concerned, there was no better way to spend a day off than being on a story adventure with friends.

Then looking at the sun, which was ever lower in the sky, and back to the happy villagers, Mirth nodded his head slowly a few times in satisfaction at the day's proceedings.

Wiseacre, still invisible to both humans and youngling fairies, was also pleased with the way things had turned out so far.

"Good job younglings" he said, knowing they wouldn't hear his words but would feel his praise.

At that moment, Mirth and his friends suddenly felt even happier and more content with the day.

Glee noticed the warm, happy look on Mirth's face and leaned towards Shimmer and Twinkle and whispered to them that he must be being loved by someone.

"Yes, us" said Twinkle.

Glee didn't mention that he meant someone else and just agreed.

"Yes we do Twinny . . . but don't tell him I said that" whispered.

Twinkle snorted in pretend annoyance.

"Boys" she snorted as if that explained everything there is to know about the two of them.

Wiseacre flew closer to Mirth, being careful not to touch him as he was invisible to the youngling fairies but could still be felt if they bumped into each other.

When he was as close as he could get without touching, he strained forward and whispered in his ear "I think that's enough mischief for one day" then quickly pulled back and flew higher again.

Mirth flew off the edge of the bird table and hovered facing his friends.

"All this picnicking has made me hungry. I think it's home time" he declared.

Twinkle laughed at this.

"You mean you didn't get a bellyful after kissing that cute fairy cake?"

"I did" answered Mirth with a grin. Then, "but I need some good old fairy folk food."

All three nodded at the mere mention of fairy folk food and as was the habit with fairies, they all looked at the sun, bowing in the autumn sky, and felt drawn to their home in the west.

Mirth left them and flew to his children to say his goodbyes. After giving some encouragement and saying a felt but not heard farewell to Oliver and his brothers David and Jonathan, Mirth flew upwards in preparation for their journey home.

"Say your goodbyes and let's be off!" he called down to Glee, Shimmer and Twinkle.

Glee quickly flew towards Max and patted him on the head without stopping then flew upwards to join Mirth.

As he made the pass and swotted Max on the head, he shouted, “keep whopping Maxy.”

“Hey, he’s supposed to behave himself” protested Shimmer,

“He will Shims, but sometimes brothers and sisters need a good whopping.”

“Yes they do,” said an annoyed Twinkle as she gave Glee one of her scary stares.

Shimmer nodded her agreement at this, then after thinking for a moment she got an idea, smiled, then flew over to Vicky and whispered in her ear. She then gave Vicky a magical kiss on the top of her head before slowly hovering up to survey her final mischievous handywork of the day as she called down to her.

“Goodbye Vicky, I’ll visit you again soon” she said dramatically.

Transferring the pile of plates to one arm, Vicky awkwardly crouched to pick a buttercup. Then surprising herself and everyone else by leaning over to Chloe, she placed the buttercup under Chloe’s already golden chin.

"Hey Chloe, let's see if you like butter," she giggled.

Mrs Vauxhall looked at Mrs Saffron in apologetic amusement.

Mrs Saffron just smiled and gave Mrs Vauxhall an approving look to show she was happy that Vicky was coming out of her shell.

Samantha laughed loudest and shouted, “I think butter likes her.”

Chloe laughed at Victoria’s joke too, and more again at Samantha’s comment.

Mirth, Glee and Shimmer also giggled as they rose higher and higher.

“Come on Twinkle” Shimmer called out to her friend.

“I’m coming, wait for me” answered Twinkle even though she wasn’t following at all.

Instead, Twinkle flew over to Chloe who was still laughing with her new friend Vicky.

Twinkle sat on Chloe’s right shoulder and resting her tiny little head on both of her hands she let out a long, deep sigh.

“Ohhhh she’s so golden and shiny and bright and cute. I want to stay here foreverrrrrr” she pined to herself as she pushed out her bottom lip.

Shimmer was now sitting with Mirth and Glee all the way up on the edge of the mossy roof of Mrs Abra's house as they dangled their legs over the edge and looked down onto the garden scene.

“Come onnn Twinks, she won’t be the only one who’s bright and shiny if we don’t get home by sunset” Shimmer called down again impatiently.

Shimmer was reminding Twinkle that youngling fairies are only allowed out during the daytime because if they stay out after the sun has gone down, they change into fireflies and can’t change back.

“And fireflies don’t get to gobble fairy folk food Twinkle” lectured her big brother Mirth.

At this, Twinkle suddenly felt quite hungry, and she also didn't much like the idea of spending the rest of her days as a firefly. She did like them, but she wasn’t obsessed with them as Scintilla’s little brother Finagle was and certainly didn’t want to be one.

So, with a sad “I'm cominggggg,” she reluctantly lifted off Chloe’s shoulder and started to fly upwards before stopping again.

She gave Chloe a long goodbye kiss on the forehead. Then, squashing her right cheek against Chloe's head as hard as she could, she spread her arms wide to hug her even though it was like trying to hug a wall as Chloe's head was way too big for Twinkle to wrap her arms around.

Finally, she reluctantly detached herself from Choe's shining, golden head and rose, slowly flying backwards and upwards, to join her friends.

As she settled alongside Shimmer on the edge of the roof, she gazed down upon her lovely golden girl. With several slow, knowing nods of her head, she sighed one last time.

"So loveleeeee."

Twinkle's three friends were also enjoying a final view of the Cuckooers and feeling very satisfied with the goings on of the day.

Their attention then turned to their final journey of the day (or so they thought). They had flown through a rainbow, been all over the village and eventually here to Mrs Abra's back garden. So, they had to look towards the sun to get their bearings to see which way led to their home.

It wasn't far actually, just a short flight over Mrs Abra's back garden and the little stream, then over Farmer Crabtree's cow field and into the woods that spread as far to the west as could be seen from atop the house.

Now that they had said their goodbyes and were all together, they felt confident that there was plenty of time to get home as the sun still hadn't quite touched the horizon.

So, the four naughty but kind hearted youngling fairies sat for a final moment to enjoy the happy scene below and the beautiful countryside stretching out before them as they bathed in the last of the setting sun's warmth.

As soon as the sun began to kiss horizon of the far western edge of their beloved woodlands, Mirth stood up and his three friends did likewise in readiness to set off.

Mirth, Glee, Shimmer and Twinkle all turned their gaze longingly in the direction of the setting sun. As it drew them westward, they leaned forward and floated up and away from the roof and set off for home.

CHAPTER 50

# Home Time

As the four fairies had said their goodbyes to their children, some of the humans were saying goodbye to each other.

"I better be getting back to Mrs Evans," said Mr Evans.

Then, with a mischievous look all of his own, he added, "she'll be wanting to know about all the comings and goings of the day, and I won't get a moment's peace until she's up to speed."

Doctor Clayton was standing somewhat behind Mr Evans, and as he met Mr Saffron's eye, he ducked his head slightly and bit his lip to prevent his smile from becoming laughter. They both well knew that it would be Mr Evans who would be pestering Mrs Evans to listen as he regaled her with a detailed story of the goings on.

Mr Saffron was facing Mr Evans so couldn't hide his involuntary smile. As he was a very happy person and smiled often, he was able to get away with his usual friendly smile suddenly transforming into an amused grin.

Mr Evans was none the wiser at the reason for his amusement. However, Mr Saffron did have to suppress the added urge to laugh when he caught sight of the doctor biting his lip.

Despite being stiff and creaky due to sitting on the grass during the picnic, Mr Evans crouched to pick up some plates from the picnic blanket to help the children in clearing away. As he did, he caught sight of all the colourfully flowering Saffron plants bordering Mrs Abra's lawn on all sides.

After struggling back up with stacked bowls in his left hand and the fingers of his other hand in three beakers, he turned to Mrs Abra.

"You really do keep a wonderful garden Mrs Abra. Would I be right in guessing these flowers to be Saffrons? And no need to guess where they came from" he said.

"Thank you Mr Evans. Yes, aren't they lovely," answered Mrs Abra with pride.

"I only gave Mrs Abra one. She gave it plenty love and now there's a hundred" said Mr Saffron in appreciation of Mrs Abra's gardening talent.

"Looks like more than an-undred to me" replied Mr Evans as he continued admiring the lavender blue borders on each side of the lawn.

"Autumn has always been my favourite time of the year, and saffrons flower late so they bring a lot of colour to the season" said Mrs Abra. Then, "I still have some potted, do let me give you one to take home for Mrs Evans."

"Oh she would like that Mrs Abra. That's very kind of you. And erm, if there's any of your delicious cake still going then, might I also take her a slice. Or, ahem two?" he asked sheepishly.

"Not at all Mr Evans" replied Mrs Abra now struggling herself not to laugh. "Just a moment."

Mrs Abra then strode over to her greenhouse, stepped inside for a moment, then reappeared with a potted saffron plant in early bloom.

"Here you are, it's just coming out so you and Mrs

Evans can enjoy the flowering."

Mr Evans took the plant gratefully as Mrs Abra placed it gently in the top bowl of the stack he was carrying.

The flowering part of the saffron plant was level with his face but a little too close to focus on. He puffed out his chest and tried to hold the bowls further way so he could admire it.

A little further in front of him were Oliver, Max Victoria and Chloe. As they had sat together for the photograph, they were now stood in a little cluster talking.

Mr Evans looked from the four children, back to the flowering saffron plant he was holding. He was amazed to observe that the plant had a green stalk, bluish petals, red stigma and within, golden seeds.

He was amazed at the colour match between the children and the plant but, unusual for him, and as with his observation of the colour pattern of the picnic blanket, he didn't say anything. He just looked in wonder as his eyes narrowed slightly and his eyebrows seemed ready to do a synchronised dive into the saffron plant.

Nodding his head in understanding and amazement, both Mrs Abra and Mr Saffron took his awed expression to be simple appreciation for the beauty of the plant.

As that was indeed the case, or part of it, he left it at that and just enjoyed the magic of the moment.

All the adults were saying their goodbyes and getting ready to head back to their own homes, but the goodbyes had a way of stretching into happy conversations as if they were reluctant to part. As they talked, the younger children started to become restless.

Doctor Clayton and Nurse Walton finally broke off from the others as they had to drive back to their clinic in

Plumton.

Mrs Abra walked along with them before Mr Saffron turned to Nurse Walton in eagerness to fulfil the doctor's earlier prediction.

"Nurse, could I delay you for just a moment. I can't let a new friend of Cuckoo Village leave without something to take with you."

Nurse Walton knew there was a flowering plant of some kind incoming, and she eagerly accepted his offer.

"Oh that's very kind of you Mr Saffron, thank you."

"I'll just pop into my greenhouse. I've got something that will be a good reminder of such a special day."

Without waiting for a reply, he darted ahead and disappeared down the path that winded around Mrs Abra's house and onto the foot path they had all come along.

Doctor Clayton smiled at Nurse Walton, showing that he had no doubt at all that his prediction would come true.

Nurse Walton gave the doctor a smile of appreciation at his fortune telling success.

"When you know people, you know the future" he said.

Although this sounded odd, in a mysterious way it also made sense to her.

Mrs Abra also smiled at this. Then she had a thought and as they were a little apart from the children, she used Nurse Walton's Christian name for the first time.

"Jenny, I do believe Mr Saffron actually meant it was a special day because it was your first visit to Cuckoo Village rather than the goings on of the day" she said as if she had discovered something wonderful.

"Well, it certainly is that" she replied feeling genuinely happy about seeing the village and meeting the Cuckooers.

Then she added "and the 'goings on' made it doubly special."

Doctor Clayton nodded in agreement as, in no hurry to leave, the three of them walked slowly towards the house. They passed through the house instead of taking the path around it as the Mr Saffron had done. The doctor had left his doctor's bag in the front hallway and needed to pick it up before they headed to his Moris Minor for the trip back to Plumton.

The three of them passed through the kitchen and living room, then reached the entrance hall which led to the still open front door.

As the doctor paused to pick up his bag, an old, framed photograph on the wall at the bottom of the stairs caught Nurse Walton's eye and she stopped to examine it.

The picture was the back garden they had just left. In it, there were a little boy and girl sitting in the sunshine on a picnic blanket. They were holding what appeared to be sandwiches and waving them in the air as they grinned happily at the photographer.

Nurse Walton turned to Mrs Abra.

"Are these your children?" she asked.

"Oh no, 'these' are their mother and uncle," she answered cryptically with a grin much like that of the sandwich waving girl in the picture.

Nurse Walton thought for a moment then, nodding once slowly, she gave a delighted "ahhh."

"The original Cuckoo picnickers" said the doctor as he looked at his sister.

"Still going strong" answered Mrs Abra. Then she added, "you know, speaking of memories, I've had a strong feeling of deja-vu all day."

Doctor Clayton raised his eyebrows with great interest, saying "so have . . ." but was cut off as a gaggle of several noisy children excitedly pushed past them on their way out through the front door.

Then, they were through the front door themselves just in time to be greeted by an out of breath Mr Saffron who presented Nurse Walton with a potted saffron plant to rival the one Mrs Abra had given to Mr Evans – except it hadn't started to flower.

"It doesn't look like much now but will flower soon" he said as he handed her a pot of what looked like a tuft of green grass.

"Oh, it's lovely. Can I keep it indoors?" she asked.

"Yes, and it should flower soon and for about three weeks, then more will grow next year. If you take care of it, it'll produce more than you know what to do with" he encouraged.

"Like a certain someone's cakes" teased the doctor.

"Or children" laughed Mrs Abra as another gaggle steamed past them with a quick and loud "byeeee" and a belated "thanks for the picnic" after they disappeared through the front door.

As chattering and clinking noises from some of the more conscientious children could be heard from the kitchen, a still red Max Sangfroid walked past the three of them with his arm around his younger brother's shoulder.

They were deep in conversation as they made plans for play-time like it was the end of a school day; which it was. Only, they had attended a different kind of school.

Max was telling Wesley that David and his brothers were going to have a stick and leaf boat race in the stream and they should make some too. Wesley was nodding enthusiastically. He knew that enough time had passed since Max had wanted to give him a whopping and as he had completely calmed down for real, he was back to just being a big brother looking for fun.

Next, Mr Evans passed the three of them and said his goodbyes as he carried the plant Mrs Abra had given him and a napkin with two thick slices of her sponge cake.

"I ope you don't mind Mrs Abra, but Mrs Evans will never forgive me if I'm to be telling her about the wonderful picnic and not bring her some of it" he said sheepishly.

As usual, Mrs Abra was as happy that someone enjoyed her baking enough to pilfer some leftovers.

"Of course Mr Evans. And there's always more if Mrs Evans wants thirds."

# CHAPTER 51

# Going Home

The Cuckooers who had attended the great Cuckoo picnic had either said their goodbyes and headed home, were washing the dishes or had stayed chatting in the garden and were still talking in the warm, late afternoon sunshine.

Soon enough but too soon, Doctor Clayton and Nurse Walton were in the doctor's beloved old Morris Minor Traveller heading east through Cuckoo Village. Then with a goodbye honk of the horn, they disappeared and were on their way back to Plumton.

Mrs Abra stood on the pavement by Cuckoo church waving until they were out of sight. Even then, she stood smiling and looking in their for a little while longer.

Folding her arms, she looked down at her feet and realised she was wearing her fluffy house slippers. She didn't mind though and just gave a contented sigh, then turned to walk back down the path to her lovely home. As she did, Wiseacre flew alongside her.

Instead of going through the front door with her, he said a felt, but unheard goodbye to the wise old lady of Cuckoo Village, then rose higher and higher until he was level with the front facing roof of her house.

CHAPTER 52

# Away with the Fairies

As he rose higher, Wiseacre looked down and noticed that the awning above the front door, as with the back door, was thatched in the same way as the roof. It occurred to him that he had never set a snow trap on a thatched awning before.

He wondered if the snow would slide off a thatched awning as easily as it does with tiled ones. In any case, he decided that it wouldn't be right to dump snow on an old lady, not even one as strong and good humoured as Mrs Abra. It's more fun making snowboys and snowgirls. So, he decided that one day, he would go way, way back in time and set the snow trap when there were children living here.

After all, he already planned to take the trip back to years gone by in order to complete a task of his own, and it's always nice if you can do two great things at the same time isn't it.

Before he could do the difficult magic needed to travel back in time though, Wiseacre had one small matter to attend to. So, he flew further up along the thatched roof, past the brick chimney and then down the other side.

Mirth, Glee, Shimmer and Twinkle were just then launching themselves on their journey home.

What they didn't know yet, was that although the four of them may have been done with mischief for the day, Wiseacre was not.

As he saw the four naughty fairy friends launch themselves from the roof and begin to fly westward on their way home, he caught up with them in readiness to give them a challenge of their own.

Wiseacre had decided to take Sally's excellent suggestion to 'do magic back at them'. After all, humans shouldn't be the only ones to face a challenge today. So, with that in mind, Wiseacre cast a spell on all four youngling fairies.

The spell took away their flying powers for the rest of the day. Either they would have to find a way to get home before sunset or get used to living as fireflies.

The spell Wiseacre cast on them wasn't a punishment exactly. After all, something good had come from their mischief. It was more of a lesson that playing with naughty magic not only has consequences for those who have been magicked, but also those doing the magic. Something Wiseacre had learned the hard way as a youngling fairy himself.

It came as a great shock to the four fairy friends when, just as they passed over Mrs Abra's back garden where they had joined the picnic with the Cuckooers, they all began to lose altitude.

Mirth was the first to notice it and he instantly knew the cause.

"Argh, what's happening?" called out Shimmer.

"I can't fly" said a worried Twinkle.

They were heading west and to home but when their flying powers were taken away, they just started to slowly float downwards. Then, quite suddenly, there was a gentle breeze that began to carry them away from their home as it pushed them eastward.

"I knew it, I just knew it!" Mirth proclaimed in a tone that was both triumphant at being right yet defeated at being caught.

His suspicion that a senior fairy had been involved all along was now confirmed.

Glee, Shimmer and Twinkle had never lost the ability to fly before so were quite alarmed. Shimmer let out a little whimper as she drifted ever lower and away from their woodland home.

"Ooo, goodness what's happening?" she squeaked as she reached out to take Twinkle's hand.

"It's a spell, don't worry. An oldster must have cast a 'flightless' spell on us" reassured Mirth who, due to this not being his first brush with mischief, had contingency plans for such . . . consequences.

"Aww I knew we'd get rumbled," complained Glee, disappointed but not sorry.

"Where are we going?" demanded Twinkle as they all tried their best to follow Mirth.

"Well, we can't fly home, and it would take until after sundown to walk. So, a sticky problem needs a sticky solution. I've already arranged transport for part of the way but for the rest we are just going to have to take the 'Cow Sneeze Express'" answered Mirth as he looked back and down at them with a crazed glint in his eyes.

"The 'COW SNEEZE EXPRESS'. . . Yeeee haaaaaaaaa!" hollered Glee.

With a mixture of trepidation and excitement, Mirth, Glee, Shimmer and Twinkle accepted that the day's adventure wasn't yet over. And that their journey home wouldn't be as short or easy as they expected.

The four closest of fairy friends then set their faces in

the direction the easterly breeze carried them and prepared for the challenge ahead.

"Ok, here we go" called out Mirth.

"Here we go" replied Glee, Shimmer and Twinkle.

Now, I'm sure you would like to hear the story of the adventurous journey home of the flightless fairy leader Mirth, his best friend Glee, Mirth's little sister Twinkle and Twinkle's best friend Shimmer. As well as to read about what on earth the Cow Sneeze Express is. But that story is for another time. After all, buttercups only have five petals, and you couldn't possibly fit two whole stories on just five buttercup petals now, could you?

EPILOGUE

1

# How do I do?

Having cast his spell on the four fairy friends, Wiseacre said goodbye to the present and everyone in it, and set off on his own journey in time, but not space.

As he prepared to move from the present into the past, he noticed his future-self appear from the past into the present; just in time to follow the four naughty youngling fairies to see how they managed their challenging, flightless way home.

Future Wiseacre was eager to see if any adventures they have along the way might make an interesting story to tell someday.

"How do I do?" nodded present Wiseacre just before he disappeared into the past.

"How do I do?" replied future Wiseacre just as he appeared from the past.

Neither of them wanted to chat to the other too much. After all, bumping into your past or future self can lead to some unusual outcomes. So, with those pleasantries out of the way, present and future Wiseacre went about their business.

Just before present Wiseacre disappeared from the present on his journey into the past, a large magpie flew between the two invisible senior fairies.

"Hope you don't mind if I borrow this" said present

Wiseacre as he plucked a tiny feather from the magpie's brow.

Then in an instant he was gone.

The magpie couldn't see Wiseacre, but she certainly felt a sharp pinch as a feather was plucked from just above her right eye.

A moment later, the magpie felt another pinch as future Wiseacre replaced the borrowed feather.

"Thanks Maggie, that came in handy" said an always courteous Wiseacre even though she couldn't hear him.

Then, as the magpie was flying in the same eastward direction the breeze had carried Mirth, Glee, Shimmer and Twinkle, future Wiseacre hopped aboard and rode along so he could catch up to them and enjoy their new adventure.

2

# Anywhen

Future Wiseacre had followed the puzzled youngling fairies as they ceased flying westward and instead found themselves being carried away from home by a gentle, easterly breeze.

Present Wiseacre didn't fly anywhere. Instead, he flew anywhen. Actually, he flew somewhen in particular. That is, he descended from rooftop level, down onto the picnic spot in Mrs Abra's well-kept back garden. As he did, he cast his time travel spell and moved further and further backwards in time to a particular year, month, week and day long ago.

At first, he moved slowly, just a few minutes back in time. Then ten or twenty minutes back, then an hour or so. As he went further and even faster back, everything moved backwards at double then triple then quadruple and faster speed.

All the adults and children who had already left for home now returned to Mrs Abra's house, only this time they approached the picnic spot walking backwards. Then, as they sat around the picnic blanket, they seemed to push food from their mouths into their hands then put it back onto their plate.

Wiseacre smiled as he watched well chewed, mulch came out of their mouths, form nicely into a generous triangle of cake, then placed onto their plate and finally slotted back into the wedge-shaped space of the whole cake.

When everyone had finished regurgitating all the food they had eaten and when they were done chatting away in a backwardsy language, saying things like "?legna na uoy era" Or "god a rof em gnippaws ton er'uoy," they all got up and, walking backwards, carried all the food back into the house until Wiseacre was alone in the garden.

As he moved even further and ever faster backwards in time, the sun moved east and set on the horizon beyond Plumton as a rainbow arched across the morning sky.

Eventually the rainbow and setting sun were replaced by a gossamer moon moving on its own rapid arc before the clear, moonlit sky darkened as gentle rain appearing from the ground and poured upwards to form clouds.

Soon, each day passed in reverse so quickly that the sun and the moon could no longer be seen at any one point in the sky. Instead, the sun and moon arched across the sky.

They shone overhead like alternating gold and silver rainbows stretching from horizon to horizon. Of course, that was when it wasn't cloudy and they could be seen.

Before long, he moved so quickly back in time that the days and nights flickered by at a pace too quickly to count. Then so fast that the seasons themselves flickered by as year after year after year passed in reverse.

The house remained the same with very little change apart from the back door changing colour occasionally. The well-kept lawn also changed little apart from the grass growing and being cut again and again. This gave the impression of the grass breathing as it was periodically tended to by a quick zip of a backwards walking gardener pulling a lawnmower over it too fast to see.

The flowers along the borders of the lawn flickered a variety of colours from their green stalks to whatever red, blue, yellow or other coloured flowering plant had been sewn each year.

After Wiseacre guessed that he had moved backwards in time about forty years, he slowed his journey a little and observed as a tall young mother played in the garden with her children. He was tempted to stay for a while to see if he might catch a story or two being told but decided to press on. So again, he began to speed further back in time without moving from his spot in the garden.

As he drew closer to his somewhen, he began to slow down again so that he might observe things more clearly. Things began to flicker less, and instead the sun and moon were gold and silver arches again. Then as his traveling back in time paused, the sun came to a noon halt.

This time, Wiseacre saw a young girl in an orange dress sitting alone on the cool grass as she read a book and occasionally reached out blindly for a sandwich or glass of juice that were by her side.

"There you are," he said.

When he spoke, the girl looked upwards to where he hovered above the picnic spot as if she had heard an unexpected sound. She stared curiously in his direction for a moment before looking down again to continue her reading.

"Hmphh, no stories to be heard here" said Wiseacre to himself. Then, "unless I want to read over her shoulder."

In fact, he did not want to do that as he much

preferred to hear a story told. Or if he was reading a story, he preferred to do so out loud as he read it 'to' someone.

As he was a few months off, he continued on his journey backwards in time. Again, he sped up and moved further backwards until, with an 'oops,' he noticed that in his eagerness to get to his somewhen, he had moved backwards a little too far and overshot his destination by half a year.

As he again halted his time travel, he saw that the ground was covered in snow and there was a thick white blanket on the roof of the house.

At first, he was admiring the work of the fairy who designed this particular day's snow but then realised it was him. So he laughed and congratulated himself on a good job.

He then noticed a little girl and boy dressed in winter coat, gloves, hat and scarves clomp excitedly from the house as they slammed the back door behind them in anticipation of a snowball fight and maybe building a snowman together.

Wiseacre was just about to course correct and move forwards in time to his exact somewhen, when he noticed yet another future Wiseacre hovering near the thatched, snow-covered awning over the back door.

Future Wiseacre didn't say anything, but as he noticed present Wiseacre appear at the bottom of the garden, he just looked his way and gave him a happy grin.

As the children slammed the back door in their excitement, there followed a long, soft shhhhhhhh and the two children turned back to the house and looked up to see what was making the curious sound.

Unfortunately for the children, the shhhhhh wasn't the sound of their mother telling them not to slam the door. It was the sound of fresh, fluffy snow sliding off the awning above the door and into the children's upward turned faces. There was also an invisible fairy surfing the snowslide as it piled onto them.

Before they could say anything beyond a quick "arrrrgh", the snow poured onto them and all around them until both children were completely covered and even their still open mouths were full of snow.

An excited future Wiseacre flew around them clapping then pointing at them as he laughed so hard that he lost some control of his flying and bumped into the wall several times.

"Ah, so that's how snow slides off a thatched awning" nodded present Wiseacre to himself.

After enjoying the comical scene of the snowboy and snowgirl being created, present Wiseacre left future Wiseacre and the children to it and disappeared as he nudged his way two seasons ahead in time to finally arrive at his exact somewhen.

3

# The Beginning

Wiseacre was happy to see that the somewhen he had arrived at was a cloudless, sunny day and there were no adults or children in the garden yet.

He had some important work to do and it's difficult to focus on doing important work when nearby humans are distracting him by having fun and telling each other stories.

As he was still in the air, Wiseacre moved all the way down to the spot on the ground where the picnics were usually held. This was easy to find as the grass had a large rectangle part that was flattened and paler than the rest of the well-tended, deep green lawn. This was due to the fact that people sitting on a blanket having a picnic at this very spot was a regular occurrence and Wiseacre was sure that today would not be an exception.

Wiseacre didn't settle onto the grass at the picnic spot though. Instead, he aimed for a nearby spot where a buttercup that had its golden petals proudly open as it absorbed as much of the sun's love as it was able.

He settled right in the middle of the buttercup. Its seeds were very soft and poofy, so it was actually a very comfortable place to sit.

After steadying himself from the slight sway of the buttercup, he withdrew the tiny feather that he had borrowed from the magpie. He intended to use the feather as a pen and as he didn't have any ink, he cast a writing spell on the tip.

After sitting deep in thought for a moment, he slowly leaned forward and put the feather pen to the the first five petal and began to write his story.

Thinking of a title for moment, he smiled and wrote at the top of the first petal '*A RAINBOW OVER CUCKOO VILLAGE'*.

Then he began to write his name as the author but paused and wondered if he could say he was the author when it was a true story and not something he had made up, or at least, it would be a true story one day.

He decided that even though it was a true story, he was in fact the author so he would just write the first letter of his name, so he next wrote '*By W*'.

Below that, he started writing the story of everything that he had witnessed so far that day.

In the most beautiful, ornate but clear and tiny letters, the first line of the story he wrote was *'Fairies work very, very hard'*.

With a smile, he then went on as he wrote about four mischievous, youngling fairy friends called Mirth, Glee, Shimmer and Twinkle. He wrote about their plan to use their day off to have fun playing a trick on some humans in Cuckoo Village.

He wrote about the doctor and nurse in Plumton receiving mysterious calls from Cuckoo parents. About funny Mr Evans and lovely Mrs Evans and their Quarner Shop. He wrote about the Robinson, Sangfroid, Vauxhall and Saffron families and their magical, children. About the people of Cuckoo Village paying a visit a kindly, wise old lady.

Then he wrote about Maybel, Nuzzler and Farmer Crabtree dropping by to say hello. About their lovely picnic and the funny stories that the nurse and the old lady told.

He wrote about the end of the picnic and what the children and adults had learned and how everything seemed to be sorting itself out nicely by home time.

Finally, he wrote about how Mirth, Glee, Shimmer and Twinkle were sent off on their own challenging adventure as they tried to get home without being able to fly and before sunset so they could avoid being transformed into fireflies.

Wiseacre then finished is story by writing about traveling back in time to write the story on the petals of a buttercup in the hope that some special children might find it and enjoy reading it to each other and perhaps to their own children one day.

The only thing Wiseacre didn't write about, was himself traveling back in time to write the story on the petals of a buttercup for someone to hopefully find and enjoy reading.

With the story complete, he tucked the magpie feather into his belt and hovered up in the air just above the tiny buttercup.

First, he stretched out his arms and legs in every direction after sitting and writing for so long. He then looked down at the writing-filled buttercup petals to enjoy his handy work.

Wiseacre decided that he better cast an attraction spell on the buttercup to make sure it got someone's attention. After all, it's no good working so hard to write such a magical story if no one is going to find it and read it or if it's just going to get munched by a passing cow or chomped at by some toodling wee beastie now is it?

So, as he cast the attention spell on the buttercup, he thought about how exciting it must be for someone to read such a lovely story for the first time. And although he was going to go on to new adventures, Wiseacre felt a little sad as he always does when a story comes to a close.

He remembered all the wonderful and magical stories he had read and heard. How when they were finished, he wished he had never heard them so he could read them or hear them fresh all over again.

So, he had the idea to cast a second spell on the story. It was a spell that made the reader begin to slowly forget the story once they had finished reading it. That way, when they came back to read it again, it would be a fresh and new story with all the surprises waiting for them.

Wiseacre was very pleased with how the day had gone so far. Then just as he finished casting the forgetting spell, he heard an excited shout as two little children, a boy and a girl came running out of the house carrying a green, red and blue blanket and a brown wicker picnic hamper.

Even though there was no snow on the awning above the door, it seems they had learned their lesson as they took care to close the door gently.

Then, with a contented sigh, the wise, the senior fairy nodded to himself.

"Time to be off. This is the end of my adventure with them, but just the beginning of their adventure with me" he said.

With that, he disappeared as he set off on his journey to somewhen in the future where he would follow Mirth, Mirth's best friend Glee, Mirth's little sister Shimmer and her best friend Twinkle as they struggled to get home before sunset without their flying powers and before turning into fireflies.

Wiseacre was sure there would be some exciting stories to tell from that adventure; even if he hadn't yet decided who he would tell them to.

*The beginning.*

*Dear reader:*

*Now that you have read all the way to the beginning of this story, perhaps you can help others to find it before Wiseacre's forgetting spell starts to take effect upon you.*

*You can tell your friends about the story and even send them a link to moonscion.com where they can find their very own copy of the book.*

*There will also be news of the continuing adventures of Mirth, Glee, Shimmer & Twinkle and some of their other, equally mischievous fairy friends.*

*The first being 'The Long Way Home'. This is the story of how the four flightless fairy friends struggle to get to their woodland fairy home before sunset when they will be transformed into fireflies.*

*Let's all meet there, and I will tell you more cuckoo fairy tales.*

Printed in Great Britain
by Amazon

23813301R00138